Diary of a 6th Grade NINJA

BOOK 9
Scavengers Strike Back

MARCUS EMERSON

ILLUSTRATED BY **DAVID LEE**

ALLEN&UNWIN
SYDNEY • MELBOURNE • AUCKLAND • LONDON

First published by Allen & Unwin in 2017

Allen & Unwin
83 Alexander Street
Crows Nest NSW 2065
Australia
Phone: (61 2) 8425 0100
Email: info@allenandunwin.com
Web: www.allenandunwin.com

A Cataloguing-in-Publication entry is available
from the National Library of Australia
www.trove.nla.gov.au

ISBN 978 1 76029 563 9

Cover design by Marcus Emerson and Sandra Nobes
Text design by Sandra Nobes
Cover and internal illustrations by David Lee
Set in 14 pt Adobe Garamond by Sandra Nobes
Printed and bound in Australia by Griffin Press

5 7 9 10 8 6 4

www.marcusemerson.com

MIX
Paper from
responsible sources
FSC® C009448

The paper in this book is FSC® certified.
FSC® promotes environmentally responsible,
socially beneficial and economically viable
management of the world's forests.

This one's for Finn…

In outer space, no one can hear a ninja...but I guess if that ninja were any good, no one should hear him on Earth either.

The space station's alarm was blaring so loudly that I could hardly think. The second Naoki and I appeared in the corridor, the station's security system was triggered, launching an attack of brightly coloured laser blasts.

There was no time to find cover, so I shut my eyes and used my keen ninja senses to dodge the lasers. It worked, but I knew I couldn't keep it up long. I had to shut off the security system if Naoki and I were gonna make it out alive.

'Master!' Naoki's tiny voice said, cutting through the explosions. 'The off switch! It's there! Beneath your feet!'

I looked down, surprised to see that my sidekick was right. What kind of security system had an off switch sitting out in the open? No wonder that place had problems.

I thrust my foot down, stomping on the switch.

It beeped twice, and then a robotic voice came from a hidden speaker. 'Thank you for using Lancelot's Laser Blast Security System. If ya can't beat 'em, blast 'em.'

'That was easy ...' I said. '*Too* easy.'

'Do you have a plan, master?' Naoki asked, his voice barely a whisper. 'Or ... a *master* plan?' He giggled at his own joke.

Naoki was my newest sidekick.

After my old sidekick Bennie, the T-rex, quit to play ukulele in a street band in Hawaii, Naoki was quick to apply.

Naoki's resume was just a bunch of pictures of rubbish bins that he had kicked and punched. If he were anyone else, I would've tossed out his resume, but Naoki was a *raccoon*. A *ninja* raccoon! His ninja mask was *grown* right on his *face*! *How sweet was that?*

'Yes, Naoki,' I said, floating. 'I've got a plan.'

Naoki reached out his tiny raccoon hands, and pushed himself off the wall. 'Are you gonna tell me the plan? Or is it some kind of super-secret thing that I'm just going to have to wait patiently for?'

Naoki was an amazing sidekick, but sometimes that little guy could be pushy.

I tried to play it cool, but the truth was even though I had a plan, it wasn't *much* of a plan. 'I figured we'd get into the space station, check out what's up with the power being out, and then deal with any intruders. Sound good to you?' I asked.

'Yes,' Naoki answered, but I could tell it *didn't* sound good to him.

My name is Chase Cooper, and I'm a sixth grade ninja...on a mission in deep space with a raccoon.

Naoki and I had been sent to scope out EV07. It was a space station that humans put on the edge of the Milky Way galaxy, in hopes of making contact with alien life. It bums me out to say that the space station hadn't made contact with little green beings yet.

About a week ago, all communication to and from the station had been mysteriously cut off.

We hoped the station had just lost its primary communications system and needed an upgrade, but in the real world, things were never that easy.

Naoki and I had just arrived by ninja teleportation. I'd totally tell you how to do it if I could, but you know... ninja secrets.

The power was completely out, like someone had left and shut off all the lights. But there weren't any humans aboard EV07. It was the first space station entirely run by androids.

And because the power was out, the artificial gravity wasn't working. Boxes of random spaceship parts floated weightlessly around us as well. If we were on Earth, those boxes would have easily weighed five hundred kilograms each, but since we were in space, they weighed nothing. I'd just have to remember to stay away from them when the artificial gravity came back online.

'First, we'll have to flip the switch to get some juice running through this ship's veins again,' I said. 'After that, we'll check out why the communication was cut off.'

'Perhaps the communication was cut because the power went out?' Naoki suggested.

'I dunno,' I said. 'Maybe.'

'You don't sound convinced, master,' Naoki said.

'There's just something odd about the whole thing,' I said, running my fingers along the wall as I floated towards the end of the corridor. 'This place is run by robots—'

Naoki cut me off. '*Androids*, master. You know they hate being called robots.'

'Yes, of course,' I groaned. 'I'm sorry. *Androids* were supposed to be running this place.

Their power source isn't the same as EV07's, so when the *ship* shut down, the androids should've kept going. I mean, *they* should be the ones trying to get EV07 up and runnin' again, but … have you seen any androids since we got here?'

Naoki shook his head, then said, 'Well now I'm kinda freaked out.'

'Naaah,' I said, trying to sound like I wasn't freaked out too. 'We're just at the edge of the galaxy, thousands of light-years away from a single other human being, floating down a dark hallway on an abandoned space station. It's nothing!'

'Except that sounds like a sci-fi horror movie,' Naoki whispered, his voice trembling. 'Like, where an abandoned space station comes back from a place of pure evil … with a stowaway.'

Just then, a low groaning came from inside the walls. It was the same sound a house makes in the middle of the night, when everything is dead silent, and you hear a *CREAAAAAAK* that comes from somewhere you can't see, and then you look at your dad for comfort, but he's just as wide-eyed as you are, and then you suddenly realise you have to go to the bathroom, but there's no way you're about to go all alone, and your dad shrugs and says something like, 'Eh, it's just the house settling...'

Yeah, right, Dad! I know what it sounds like when the house is settling! And a weird groaning sound *isn't* that!

Uh...Anyways...

'That sounded spooky,' I said.

'Really? You think?' Naoki said, rolling his eyes.

The groan came again, but this time from the end of the dark hallway.

Floating helplessly, I turned to the shadows only to see shadows *moving* in the shadows.

'Master!' Naoki cried. 'Shadow ninjas! Throw me!'

'On it!' I said, grabbing one of his tiny paws.

Without any gravity, Naoki was as light as a feather when I brought his body over my head, shooting him down the hallway.

Naoki rolled himself into a tight ball, keeping his knees under his stomach. I could only just see the shadow ninjas jumping back and forth through the corridor.

Zipping down the hall, Naoki shot through the shadow ninjas like a furry football, throwing his fists and feet out at the last second. But the attack didn't faze any of the ninjas. Naoki's raccoon body simply slipped through their black silhouettes like they were shadows because, well, that's *exactly* what they were.

Naoki slammed into the glass door at the end of the corridor and shouted a bunch of stuff in his native tongue that would probably be considered inappropriate if there were a translator nearby.

'Master!' Naoki said as he peered through the frosted glass door. 'Quickly! The bridge is in the next room!'

Drifting like lint in the breeze, I floated towards the end of the dark corridor, towards the shadow ninjas.

'I see a red light!' Naoki said. 'There's a computer panel at the front of the bridge! That *has* to be important, right? Like, it could start the whole station back up?'

'It sounds possible,' I said, watching the shadow ninjas bounce off the walls. In the darkness, I couldn't tell how many there were, but I was pretty sure there were more than Naoki and I could handle.

I spun around and kicked the wall closest to me to get myself moving, and I was soon flying through the hall with immense speed.

Suddenly several of the shadow ninjas came together, rising off the floor at the centre of the room, creating the shape of a person much larger than a sixth grader.

'Master!' Naoki's strained voice said. 'I've got the door open! Quick!'

'Workin' on it!' I replied just as I got to the shadowy figure standing in my way.

I shielded my face, expecting to go straight through the figure, but I guess it didn't work like that.

The shadow ninja grabbed my wrist and launched me towards the wall. Pain surged through my body as I hit it.

The shadow ninja flew towards me. He raised his fist, somehow making it grow to twice the size of a normal fist.

I couldn't reach the walls, so I kicked my feet like a dog treading water.

'Naoki!' I screamed, bicycle-kicking my legs.

If you've read anything about being in a zero-gravity environment, you know that it's nearly impossible to move in any direction unless you can push yourself off something. I could dog paddle until I puked, but I wasn't going anywhere.

All I could do was watch the shadow ninja as he delivered his finishing move.

At that moment, there was a flash of light behind the shadow ninja, back at the bridge.

That same instant, the lights above flickered to life. My body fell to the floor with a thud.

The boxes that had been floating around Naoki and me when we first arrived crashed to the floor, shaking the walls like there was an earthquake.

I jumped to my feet, ready to defend myself against the shadow ninja, but to my surprise, he wasn't there anymore. Well he wasn't *standing* anymore.

Under one of the giant boxes was the arm of my attacker, slowly vanishing into thin air like steam above a boiling pot.

'You dead?' Naoki called from down the hall.

'Just about,' I replied. 'I take it you found the lights then?'

Naoki chuckled. 'Yeah! Turns out the blinking red light *was* the right button.'

'Nice,' I said, dusting myself off as I stood up.

I joined Naoki on the bridge of the space station and studied our surroundings. Except for a few notches on the floor, everything seemed to be in tiptop shape.

EV07's bridge was a giant circle that was completely empty. Along the outside of the bridge were blinking computer panels and screens for crewmembers to work on.

In the middle of the floor was a blue glowing circle, pulsing slowly like it was breathing. The blue circle was the heart of the bridge, and created holograms of the rest of the ship's control panels in the big empty space of the bridge.

These holograms were the controls that kept EV07 running smoothly. Even though they were holograms, they felt solid. You could bump your knee on one if you weren't careful.

I walked out to the centre of the bridge,

tapping my foot on the blue circle. 'How do we get this thing to work, because I'd love to—'

A powerful light switched on from the back of the bridge, shining so bright that it was impossible to see anything.

'Naoki?' I said, squeezing my eyes shut. 'Can you see anything?'

I moved forward, but I bumped into an object that had appeared out of nowhere. The holograms on the bridge had switched on!

'Master!' Naoki's voice said. 'I'm stuck! Something's ... got me!'

'Keep talking,' I said. 'I'll follow your voice.'

'And if I speak over your friend?' another voice said from somewhere near the back of the room.

'Uh, Naoki?' I asked.

'Still here,' Naoki said. 'And that wasn't me.'

The voice of the stranger belted out a laugh. 'No, it was me!'

'Who are you?' I asked, trying to move forward, but it was impossible. My legs were stuck on something solid, but I couldn't feel anything wrapped around my body. I looked behind me at my shadow that was cast against the floor of the bridge. Holding onto the shadow of my ankles were the shadow ninjas. They were holding my own shadow down so I couldn't move!

'Someone you know very well... and someone you hardly know at all,' said the stranger. I could hear them pacing slowly back and forth.

'Yeah, okay,' I said. '*That* makes sense.'

The stranger stepped closer, but stayed hidden just outside the beam of light. He was only near enough that I could make out his shape. He was roughly the same size as me, and over his face... was a black ninja mask.

'You know,' the ninja said. 'It's almost disappointing how easy it was to lure you out here to the edge of the galaxy. I honestly thought I'd have to go through with this incredibly elaborate plan. I mean, I spent *weeks* on it! After the power went out, I was gonna go ahead and start flipping the power on and off, hoping to catch someone's attention. Then I was gonna reprogram all these robots to send video waves back to Earth, and … yadda, yadda, yadda. I won't bore you with the details.'

'So you've got me here,' I said. 'What do you want?'

The bright spotlight dimmed but didn't fully shut off. The shadow ninjas holding my ankles needed that light to cast my shadow, otherwise I'd break free from them.

The mystery ninja stepped around me, just out of my reach. I studied the bridge and saw the spotlight near the back. Along a row of the computer terminals were several porcelain cups that looked way too fancy for a bunch of androids.

'Nice tea set,' I said. 'That's a lot of pottery for a villain.'

'What?' the ninja asked. I could see his eyes through the holes in his mask, and I could tell he was smiling. 'Villains can't have nice things?'

His voice was *so* familiar, but I just couldn't place it. It was a boy's voice, which meant that

SPACE
NINJA!

(STANDING ON THE
BRIDGE OF A
PRETTY SWEET
SPACE STATION)

9.16 - 4.19 - 4.27

☰ 10.27

it wasn't the vampire queen Naomi. It definitely wasn't Wyatt either. I went through the list of kids who hated me – Jake? Nope. Sebastian? Nope. Carlyle? Nope. Mr A. Lien? Because he caught me making fun of his name one time … also nope.

'I can see the confusion in your eyes,' the ninja said, stepping towards me.

I blinked. 'Maybe because that's all you can see of my face? Duh.'

The ninja smiled. 'You know me, Chase Cooper, but you can't quite put your finger on who I am yet, can you? It's right there, isn't it? On the *tip* of your tongue, but you can't *even*!'

I said nothing, hating the fact that he could read my mind. I tried to keep my expression blank.

'I'll be honest with you,' the ninja said. 'You've looked me in the eye every single day, but you've never been able to see my *actual* eyes until now, in this space station.'

'Okaaaaay?' I said, pretty confused.

'I've lived in darkness too long,' the mystery ninja said, stepping even closer. His voice was maddeningly familiar. He reached out and pulled my mask off. 'But I'm ready to step into the light ... and go home to Earth.'

'Who are you?' I asked, feeling the cold air of EV07 on the bare skin of my face.

'Out of all the enemies you've ever had,' the ninja went on, 'I'm by far your worst.

Surprisingly, I've been your worst enemy since you first became a ninja all those thousands of years ago in the woods...'

'Uh, no?' I said, trying to shake my ankles free from the shadow ninjas at my feet. 'Pretty sure Wyatt was the bad guy back then. If I had some sort of unofficial foe, I'd probably know about it, right?'

'Wrong,' the ninja said coldly.

'And y'know what else? Even if you *do* make it back to Earth,' I said, 'they'll lock you up the instant you get there! All I have to do is send one video wave back to my bosses, and they'll put an alert out for you!'

'But Chase,' the ninja said, stepping so close that his face was only a foot away from mine. 'How are they gonna lock *me* up...when *I'm* the one who sent the video wave in the first place?'

The ninja grabbed the top of his mask. With a snap of his wrist, he yanked his ninja mask off his face.

The boy under the mask... the one whose voice was so familiar...

... was *me.*

I was staring, dumbfounded, at my own face as he smiled an evil smile back at me.

'Mind. Blown,' Naoki stated from across the room. 'Chase, he must be a clone! Your *evil* clone!'

'But that's impossible!' I said. 'All the way out here at the edge of the galaxy? If he were a clone of me, where'd he even get the *hair*?'

Naoki looked at me, puzzled. The ninja with my face did the same thing.

'You mean, like, the hair they used to clone you?' Naoki asked.

'No,' I said. 'The hair that's sitting on top of his head right now.'

The ninja with my face ran his fingers through his thick head of hair. '*This* hair?'

'Yeah!' I said. 'If you're my clone, then where'd you even get that?'

Naoki and my evil clone looked at each other. Naoki shrugged.

'You don't really understand how cloning works, do you?' the ninja asked.

I pouted, but, like, a *heroic* pout. 'Yuh-huh.'

My evil clone walked around me slowly. 'You're broken, Chase. You've been cracked over and over, and now you're barely able to keep yourself together anymore.'

'So that's it?' I asked. 'You brought me here to break me?'

The clone nodded. 'I'm the perfect version of you! Flawless and *awesome*. I'm going to replace you, and by the time anyone realises I'm *not* you, the world will already be mine. Humanity will bow before my ninja fist!'

'Pretty sure my friends will know something's up because of that goatee,' I huffed.

My clone stopped and narrowed his eyes at me. 'You know I can shave it off, right?'

'Dangit!' I grunted. 'You know you're in a boatload of trouble when I get free from these shadow ninjas, right?'

'Then I suppose it's time for me to relieve you from your duty...' the clone said, '...of *living*.'

'He said *doodie*!' Naoki laughed.

'Dude! Not helping!' I shouted. I was beginning to wonder whether a raccoon was a poor choice of sidekick.

In a flash of black, my evil clone spun away from me and floated in the air for a full second, charging himself up. And then he tightened his fists and threw his finishing move.

Raising my hands, I did my best to block the attack, but I was too late. His punch landed square on my cheek...

But to my surprise, it barely hurt. Actually, it

was more annoying than painful. It was kind of like a piece of toast had hit me in the face.

Wait, what?

I wasn't on some abandoned space station on the edge of the galaxy. I was in the school cafeteria, staring at a piece of toast that was on the table in front of me.

Someone from the next table next had thrown it, and that entire table of kids was snickering and pointing at me.

And then another bit of toast came from the table, sailing high in the air until landing right on top of my head.

Great. What a way to start the week.

Monday.
The cafeteria.

I had got to school a little early, so I thought it would be nice to grab some breakfast. Most of the time, breakfast in the cafeteria was pretty quiet, but for some reason that morning a couple of kids thought it'd be funny to chuck food at me.

I think they were still mad about the newsletter that came out a week or so back – the one the Scavengers printed with secrets about every sixth grader in the school. And of course, the Scavengers made it look like I was behind the newsletter.

Since I didn't feel like being a target for the kids at the next table, I scooped up my tray and headed for the rubbish bin at the side of the cafeteria.

I caught a glimpse of Naomi at the other end of the lunchroom. She was sitting alone, but she didn't notice me. Good thing too, because I probably would've looked away as soon as she did, which was the obvious clue that someone was staring at you.

For the past week, it was like some secret part of my brain would find Naomi before I realised it. Whenever she was around, I knew exactly where she was before even looking at her. Sometimes I imagined a giant carnival sign with her name on it, hovering over her head, trying to get my attention.

Naomi was eating a sausage roll. An orange juice was on the table in front of her, next to a small cup that looked like something from a tea party set.

Naomi used to be one of my best friends. She was a strong member of my ninja clan, and we

had fun together even when it wasn't about ninja stuff. But that all ended when she turned out to be a spy for the bad guys. She had been lying to me since the first week of school, pretending to be one of my ninjas – and my friend.

The real bummer though? Naomi might've been a 'bad guy', but I still missed her as a friend. Sure, she might've been playing me from the start, but we had some real laughs together.

When I got to the rubbish bin, I tipped my tray and banged it against the side of the plastic barrel. I watched all my food plop down into the depths of nastiness with a gross *SPLORT*.

'Seriously?' a boy said from behind me. 'You hardly ate any of that food! You're just gonna waste it like that? Why even bother getting breakfast if all you're gonna do is take a bite and throw the rest out?'

The boy's name was Jesse, and he was a volunteer cashier for the kitchen. Sixth graders were allowed to volunteer for school positions like that if their grades were good enough.

'Sorry, man,' I said, feeling guilty. I didn't want to explain that *my* breakfast was already digesting in my belly. I had just thrown out the toast that had been chucked at me.

Jesse shook his head. 'No, *I'm* sorry,' he said, nudging me aside as he grabbed the sides of the black rubbish bag that lined the barrel. 'Maybe next time, *don't* buy so much toast.'

I didn't feel like arguing. 'Righto, captain.'

He looked at me, annoyed. And then got back to pulling the rubbish bag from the bin.

I set my tray on the kitchen counter, and headed for the school lobby. I had a few minutes to try and find my friends.

 **Monday.**
The lobby.

Out in the lobby, kids were pushing through
the front doors, trying to escape the freezing
cold weather outside. The temperature had
dropped over the weekend, which meant it was
officially time for snowballs and winter coats.

A bunch of kids were clumped together just
inside the building, staring up at the brand new
statue of (dead) President James Buchanan.

But this statue was not like any other statue.
The rumour spreading across the earballs of
everyone in school was that a video game
company had gone out of business, and had

27

sold everything in their studio for super cheap, including ginormous statues of heroes from their last game.

Buchanan School bought one of the statues, and replaced the head of the video game character with the head of James Buchanan. Which meant our statue was a *super* jacked, and I mean *ripped*, James Buchanan next to a giant grizzly bear.

The president was wearing a fur loincloth and holding a tiny pole with a little school flag on it.

'James Buchanan looks like a dude who knew how to party,' Zoe said from next to me. 'Or fight off an army of the undead. Either-or.'

Zoe is my cousin. She's also the school president.

'Right?' I said, admiring the huge statue. It was over two-and-a-half metres high. 'Is he supposed to be fighting that bear, or is that a pet bear?'

'I think it's his pet,' Zoe replied.

'What a goofy thing to have in our lobby,' Faith said from my other side.

'So ...' I said. 'Learn any cool ninja moves lately?'

Faith was one of my best friends, but she was also the white ninja! Too bad anytime I tried bringing it up in conversation, she completely ignored me as if I wasn't even there.

Faith pressed her lips together and said, 'That bear is freakin' me out, man.'

See? She totes ignored me.

'Is it the bear's hairstyle?' Faith asked. Then she leaned forward and yelled, 'Get a haircut, ya yak!'

'That's a bear,' I said. 'Not a yak.'

Faith rubbed the bridge of her nose. 'I know, dude. It was a joke.'

'Well, it wasn't very funny!' I said playfully. 'How do you think yaks feel when you confuse them with bears?'

'Dude,' Faith sighed. 'Yaks don't care.'

'They don't care?' I said. 'That's re*donk*ulous! Of course they care!'

'Quit makin' up words, Cooper!' Faith snipped.

Zoe finally leaned over. 'Children,' she

scolded. 'Maybe try using your inside voices? And what's all this talk about donkey lips?'

'Re-*donk*-u-lous,' I said slowly. 'Not donkey lips.'

'Why're you makin' up words?' Zoe said.

'Forget it,' I groaned.

That's when Faith started bouncing her shoulders to a silent beat. Zoe stared into my eyes as her shoulders started to bounce too. Then, with her lips pressed tight ... she started beatboxing.

'Yak, yak, yak, yak, yakkity yak, yak,' Faith rapped like she was in a rap battle. 'Attack of the wacky yak, wacky tacky yakky yak. The yak shack! Severe lack of yak back! Yo, that yak is whack, Jack! Yak is the brand new black, mack! We're the yak pack!'

Zoe and Faith both crossed their arms at me when they were finished.

I burst out laughing. 'Did you guys plan that or something?' I asked. 'Is that why you made the joke about the yak? So that you could break into a yak rap?'

Faith giggled. 'Totes,' she said. 'It was Zoe's idea. Next, we're gonna be able to slide into a smooth breakdance at the drop of a hat.'

'It's gonna be suh-weeeeeeeeet!' Zoe said, shutting her eyes.

I wasn't sure exactly what was happening, but it was *awesome*. It was possible that Zoe was going to grow up to be weirder than me.

Zoe looked at me, and got serious. 'You know we've got that meeting in a few minutes, right? You didn't forget, did you?'

'No way, dude!' I said. 'I didn't forget at all!'

'Cool,' Zoe said. 'Wait, you're not doing that thing where you say, "No way, dude," just to make me happy because you actually really did forget about the meeting?'

'No!' I said.

'He forgot,' Faith laughed.

Zoe jabbed my chest. 'Ninjas. Don't. Forget.'

'Sure they do!' I said. 'You're thinking of elephants. And, like, people with grudges. And also the people you owe money.'

I could tell that Zoe was serious. She was

pretty stressed, and after everything that she had been through, I felt bad for giving her a hard time. She had enough to worry about, and I didn't need to add to her list.

In fact, I was probably going to leave her alone for most of the week. When Zoe's got a lot on her plate, it's best to steer clear of her until *she* comes looking for *you*.

Zoe slapped my book bag. 'Alright, then. Good talk,' she said. 'See ya in a few minutes.' And then her voice turned all dark. '*Don't forget!*'

'*Oh my god*, I won't!' I said.

Faith pointed at me with her finger, and wheezed, '*Don't forget, Chase Cooooooper.*'

'It sounds like you're telling me not to forget about Chase Cooper,' I joked.

Faith's eyes darted back and forth. She ignored my comment, and wheezed again. '*Cooooooooper…*'

After that, Zoe and Faith disappeared into the sea of students rushing to homeroom.

Glancing at the clock above the cafeteria

doors, I saw that I didn't have time to get to my locker before school started. No biggie. I could hit it later.

I turned on the ball of my foot and made my way through the crowd of students gathered in the lobby, admiring the super-buff President Buchanan.

Brayden was on the edge of the crowd, waiting for me with Slug and Gidget. Those three kids were the only ones in my ninja clan now, and I wouldn't have it any other way.

'Yo,' Brayden said, tilting his head. Brayden is one of my best friends. I know he has my back no matter what. Like, if aliens ever invade the planet, Brayden and I will roam the country as a team, trying to take it back from them.

Gidget had her phone pointed at the statue. She snapped a photo and started tapping on her phone.

Slug was standing with his hands stuffed into his pockets and his elbows locked. His head was tilted back, and his eyes were shut. I couldn't tell if he was sleeping or just giving his eyes a break.

'What's the plan for today, boss?' Gidget asked without looking up from her phone.

'No plan,' I said. 'I'm thinking about laying low this week. This month has been the worst. It'll be nice to take a break, y'know?'

Slug raised his eyebrows. I guess he *wasn't* sleeping. 'Welllllll,' he said. 'It's only Monday. There's plenty of time for things to go south.'

'Ever the pessimist,' Gidget said.

'Am not!' Slug said defensively. 'Unless that's a good thing? What's it mean?'

Gidget rolled her eyes. 'It means you always think the worst is going to happen.'

'Nuh-uh!' Slug said, and then paused. 'You're talking about that meteor that's supposed to pass by the Earth at the end of the year? If it's *pessimist* for me to buy a bunch of canned goods and bottled water because a giant space boulder might destroy mankind, then alright, maybe I'm being *pessimist!*'

'Pessimis*tic*,' Gidget said, correcting her brother. 'You're not even saying the word right.'

'That's because I just learned it!' Slug said. 'Anyway, I'm the opposite of a pessimist because I think *dying* when a meteor hits is probably the *best* thing – survivors will be dealing with mutants and zombies and, like, killer robots and other junk!'

'*Optimist*,' Gidget said. 'The opposite of a pessimist is an optimist.'

Slug groaned. 'Stop schooling me before school, Gidget. Mum told you not to do that.'

'Mum's not here,' Gidget replied.

Slug made a funny face, raising his eyebrows and leaning his head over. 'Then I'll *tell* on you.'

Finally, Brayden put an end to the whole thing. 'Guys,' he said, shocked. 'Seriously, you two are acting like brother and sister!'

Gidget and Slug both stared at Brayden, like, 'Duh!'

'Oh, right,' Brayden said. 'Twins.'

'So this?' I said, pointing at the statue. 'This is pretty sweet, huh?'

Gidget looked up. 'Was President Buchanan a secret superhero?'

'Only in my dreams,' I joked.

'You dream about him?' Slug asked.

'Yes!' I said. 'I mean, no. I mean, never mind. It's a long story and I don't wanna talk about it.'

'Really?' Gidget said. 'Because that's *all* I wanna talk about now.'

I rolled my eyes. 'It was *one time*, okay? Let's move on.'

'Whatever, man,' Slug said. 'Dude was buff, that's for sure.'

'Look at the neck,' I said. 'See that line?'

Slug and Gidget both squinted at the statue.

'You can tell the body was from somewhere else,' I said. 'They attached the head afterwards.'

'Whoa,' Slug said. 'He's like some kind of monster or something then ... wait—'

'Don't say it,' Gidget said, cutting him off. Slug was about to say something re*donk*ulous, and she knew it.

'What if this *was* how Buchanan really looked?' Slug suggested. 'What if all the other statues and paintings of him got it wrong? What if he was really some kind of super freaky monster that had a head transplant? I mean, of course it would've been *after* he was the president, but still!'

Brayden stared at Slug. 'So much awesome in that idea,' he said.

Yup, Brayden, the professional monster hunter, would totes agree with Slug on that.

'I bet the president used his power to force a mad scientist to perform the operation,' Brayden said. 'He did it so he could live forever!'

38

'Oh!' Slug said, struck with an idea. 'And that bear is the mad scientist! Like, after Buchanan got his jacked body, the scientist put his own brain into the bear's head!'

'The scientist... put his own brain into the bear's head?' I asked. 'Like, the scientist performed that operation... on himself?'

'Duh,' Slug said. 'Anyone who could successfully transplant a human head could easily put their own brain into something else.'

Gidget burst out laughing. 'Can you guys hear yourselves right now? Are you for real?'

Brayden and Slug ignored her.

'And they fought crime after midnight!' Brayden said.

'Of course they did,' Slug said. 'What else would they do?'

Gidget shook her head. I'm not sure why she was surprised at what Brayden and Slug were saying. I definitely wasn't.

'Heads up,' Brayden said as his face turned serious. 'Trouble at two o'clock.'

'Two o'clock?' Slug questioned. 'What happens at two?'

'No, dude,' Brayden sighed. 'Two o'clock, like the direction.'

'Huh?' Slug said, spinning in a circle.

Gidget groaned, slipped her phone back into her front pocket, and grabbed her brother's shoulders, pointing him in the right direction.

On the other side of the statue was Naomi, and she was heading our way. My ninja clan knew all about what happened between Naomi and me. I think even Faith knew, but Zoe was clueless. She had no idea what was going on with Naomi or the Scavengers, and I hoped to keep it that way. The less she knew, the better, I thought.

Last week, Naomi told me that the leader of the Scavengers had it in for me. The Scavengers are a group of kids that collect every tidbit of information on every kid, and use it to control the school. They've got all the dirt on everyone. You know that note from your BFF that you tossed in the bin during homeroom? The

Scavengers picked it up. And the conversation about the girl you have a crush on? A Scavenger overheard it. And how about the break-up note you got? Yup ... it doesn't matter how much you tore it up, the Scavengers taped it back together.

The Scavengers were bad kids, and it turned out they had way more members than I thought. Naomi was their leader, but that was just for the *sixth-grade* Scavengers. There were seventh- and eighth-grade Scavengers too. And at the very top was a kid named Victor.

I've never met Victor before, and I wanted to keep it that way. I don't know what he had planned for me, but it couldn't be good.

'Have they tried talking to you again?' Brayden asked. 'The Scavengers, I mean.'

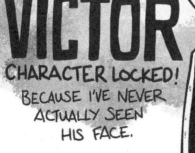

VICTOR
CHARACTER LOCKED!
BECAUSE I'VE NEVER
ACTUALLY SEEN
HIS FACE.

'Not yet,' I said. 'But I *wish* they would. It's like waiting for someone to make a move in chess – just go already! Am I right?' I joked.

Brayden nodded, staring off into space like he'd just had a brilliant idea.

'Hey,' Naomi said as she walked by.

Just then, Wyatt passed in the opposite direction. Surprisingly, he didn't even say anything mean.

Wyatt was the Lex Luthor to my Superman. (I'm Superman, duh.) He was the leader of the red ninja clan, and had been nothing but a fly in my soup since the beginning of the year. If something evil was being cooked up, you'd better believe Wyatt was the chef.

'Hey!' I called out to Wyatt, confused that he was just ignoring me like that. 'What gives?'

Why did I do that? He would've just walked by and everything would've been cool!

Wyatt turned towards me, and stared confused, like he wasn't even sure who I was. His eyes darted back and forth like he was expecting a trap to come down on him.

Then he just *walked away*.

'That was weird,' Gidget said.

'Yeah,' I replied. 'Why didn't he say anything?'

Gidget jabbed my arm. 'No,' she said angrily. '*You* were being weird! Do you *want* him to mess with you?'

Brayden and Slug laughed, and I shrugged.

After we said our goodbyes, I headed down the hall. I didn't want to be late to Zoe's meeting, or I'd never hear the end of it.

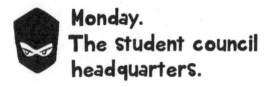

Monday.
The student council
headquarters.

The student council headquarters was one of the home economics classrooms. It was one of the only rooms that didn't have a class in it during homeroom. Zoe just called it the student council headquarters because it sounded better.

The classroom had four kitchen islands, each with six stools at it, and a sink on one end. Zoe was leaning against the counter closest to the door. Dani, Colin and Bounty, the other three members of student council, were on stools on the other three sides of the island, scribbling notes. Last week, Dani helped Wyatt cheat in the Spirit Week games. She was almost suspended from the student council, but since she owned up and apologised, Zoe gave her a second chance. Zoe's awesome like that.

Principal Davis was there too, standing against one of the other islands.

'Okay,' Zoe said, glancing at me as I took a seat on one of the stools behind her. 'So we've got an ice-cream guy, a pizza guy, a weird pretzel guy named Teddy, a funnel cake guy, and a guy who specialises in frying any kind of junk food you bring him. Are we good for food then?'

'I think so,' Dani said. 'They'll be here to set up after school on Friday.'

'Cool beans,' Zoe said, and then she pointed at Bounty. 'Where are we at with the games?'

Bounty tapped his pencil and stuttered something nobody really understood.

'Dude,' Zoe said with a chill voice. She always used a calm tone when she was about to get serious. 'The Buchanan Bash is *this* Friday.

You knew this a couple of weeks ago and had plenty of time to plan. Please tell me you didn't drop the ball on this, because that would literally *stop* my heart. Is that what you want, Bounty? Do you want me to die?'

Bounty couldn't hold it in anymore and laughed. 'No, I'm kidding! We're good. All the games are good to go for Friday. We have most of the stuff for the games in the school storage, we just need parents to volunteer to run them.'

'Are you sure having a "fun fair" isn't just for first graders?' Colin moaned.

'It's not a "fun fair", it's the Buchanan Bash,' Zoe said firmly. 'I'm not about to let my presidency be boring. The sixth graders have been through way too much to not throw them a huge party. You know you're gonna love it, and what's not to love? Games? Prizes? Music? Junk food? This party is gonna be face-meltingly good! At the end of the night, we'll all be confused about who anyone is because our faces will have melted off, and— Nope, y'know what? Too far. Melting faces was too far.'

Everyone laughed, including Principal Davis.

Zoe turned to me. 'How about you, Chase? How's your thing coming along?'

'Good! It's good!' I said.

Zoe was letting me build a giant entrance to the Bash. It would be right inside the lobby, next to body-builder James Buchanan.

I spent most of the weekend building the main part of it, but was going to use the rest of the week to add the final details. My dad helped me bring it to school earlier that morning, and at that moment, it was sitting in the storage garage that Bounty had talked about earlier.

Zoe grinned. 'Well, where is it? I wanna see!'

I shook my head. 'Nope,' I said. 'It's not done yet! I said you can see it when it's done!'

'Okay,' Zoe said, 'but you know that the Bash is in five days, right? Like, your thing needs to be done *before* the end of the week.'

'Yeeessss,' I drawled, rolling my eyes. 'I knowwwww.'

'Okay,' she said. 'It's just that I know how

you misunderstand things sometimes.'

'No, I don't!' I said defensively. 'Oh, you're talking about that *one* time, aren't you? Okay fine, *one* time.'

'Chase is doing a fine job with it, Zoe,' Principal Davis said. 'I'm so confident you'll love it that we'll unveil it to the entire school on Friday morning during the assembly for the Bash. Right there in the cafeteria.'

'Seriously?' I asked, feeling my blood pump faster.

'Seriously,' Principal Davis repeated.

Zoe sighed. 'As long as you—'

The door swung open and slammed against the counter behind it. Jesse, the kitchen volunteer, stood there with sweat on his brow and grease on his sleeves.

'Principal Davis!' he shrieked as he leaned into the room. 'Come quick! There's been an *incident*!'

Everyone in the room gasped. Zoe even choked on some spit. She clutched at her chest and coughed loudly.

'An incident?' Principal Davis said, concerned.

'Yes!' Jesse continued. 'An incident so epic that our hearts will bleed! Someone's taken James Buchanan's head!'

I looked at Zoe, who looked at me, and then the rest of the student council.

'Wait, wait, wait,' Principal Davis said, patting at the air in front of him. 'Was anyone actually hurt?'

Jesse grew frustrated. 'Yes, Principal Davis! Our *feelings* were hurt by this horrible, awful crime!'

The principal let his body rest against the counter, breathing a sigh of relief. 'Okay, so nobody *actually* got hurt. I swear you kids are going to give me a heart attack.'

 **Monday.
The lobby.**

We all followed Principal Davis back to the school lobby – the scene of the crime.

The new statue was headless.

Principal Davis silently studied the broken statue. He was staring at the spot where the head had been cracked off.

'Look at the floor,' I said, pointing around my shoes. 'There's some white dust where the head must've landed, but … it's gone.'

'This is bad,' Zoe said. 'The Bash is on Friday. Parents are going to come with their kids, and when they see this …'

Principal Davis finally spoke. 'There's no way we can get a replacement head for the statue in five days. It took *months* to get the last one.'

After some more grumbling, Principal Davis headed to the front office saying something about making phone calls and how he'd rather be on a beach in Hawaii 'swimming it up'.

Bounty, Dani and Colin continued to study the powder on the floor and give their two cents about the whole thing to each other. I took a seat on one of the benches by the front entrance to the school.

'Who would do such an awful thing?' Zoe asked, sitting next to me. 'Pranks like this are so lame.'

I shrugged. 'Maybe it was just an accident.'

'Riiiiight,' Zoe said. 'Like *anything* at this school is ever *just* an accident. This school is cursed, and I bet in a hundred years when our great-great-grandkids go here, they'll be dealing with their own set of ridiculous problems like this.'

'You think our great-great-grandkids will go to this school?' I said, excited at the thought.

'Sure, why not?' Zoe said nonchalantly.

'You think this will even be a school still? In the year 2117?' I asked.

'This was a school a hundred years ago, why wouldn't it be a school in another hundred?' Zoe said.

I scratched the back of my neck. 'I should start leaving little clues around the building for my great-great-grandkid to find,' I said. 'How *amazing* would that be? Like, I can send him messages from the past!'

Zoe gave me a look like I'd gone too far, even for me.

'What?' I laughed. 'I'm just sayin' that if I had to go around finding a bunch of stuff from our dead great-great-grandparents, it would rock my socks off!'

'You're such a weirdo sometimes,' Zoe grinned with a half smile.

'Hey, so uh…' I coughed awkwardly. 'Faith told me that you and Gavin broke up. Are you…I mean, do you…' I trailed off.

Zoe's eyes looked sad but she gave me a quick smile. 'I'm okay. It's kind of a bummer.' She shrugged.

'Yeah, totes,' I said. 'Well if you wanna…you know, whatever.'

Zoe laughed. 'I know, thanks Chase. You're the best cousin.' She gave me a quick hug, then turned back to the statue. 'You gonna look into this prank then? The case of the missing head?'

I still had to finish my project for the Bash, and with it being only a few days away, I didn't have much time to run around the halls questioning kids.

And it sure didn't seem like the prank had anything to do with my ninja clan, so I felt like things were safe there too. Best to keep things normal rather than stir up trouble where there wasn't any.

'Nah,' I said at last. 'I think I can pass on this one. A kid needs a break every now and then, right? Besides, I think Davis has it under control.'

'Good,' Zoe said. 'For the record, I'm glad you're letting the adults handle this. I think it's time for you to just start enjoying sixth grade like a normal eleven-year old.'

Yup, that was me...a *normal* eleven-year old.

 **Monday.
Lunch.**

The rest of the morning went, as swimmers
would say, swimmingly. Or maybe fish would
say that. But do fish know that they're
swimming? Oh, man ... *do fish know that they're
swimming?* That's gonna bug me for the rest of
my life.

Most kids were upset that someone had
stolen Buchanan's head. Even though the statue
was pretty goofy, it was *our* goofy statue.

I was standing in the lunch line, waiting for
my turn to pay for the pile of stuff on my tray
that the school called food. Seriously, Salisbury

steak is just chunks of meat slathered in 'gravy', which may or may not be mud, on a piece of bread. Urgh.

Jesse was working the register when I got to the front of the line. He was wearing an apron that had a badge on it that said, 'Ask me about our tomatoes'.

'What's up with your tomatoes?' I asked, handing Jesse my cash.

'I wish people would stop asking me that,' Jesse sighed as he jabbed at some of the buttons on the register. 'Seriously, kids ask me that *every single day*, and it's getting on my nerves.'

'Maybe stop wearing the badge?' I suggested.

Jesse fiddled some more with the register, looking around like he was nervous or something.

'Oh, dude,' I said, feeling bad. 'I don't really care about your tomatoes. It was a joke.'

The lights on the cash register blipped, and then the small screen on top of it said, 'FREE LUNCH'.

Jesse groaned, tilting his head back.

'Free lunch?' I said.

'The register's been acting like this all day,' Jesse said. 'It's some kind of glitch that keeps ringing up free lunches.' He slammed his fist on top of the machine. 'Bad register! No! Bad!'

'Sweet!' I said. 'Can I get my money back?'

Jesse barked out a sarcastic laugh. 'Um, no,' he said as he reached into his apron pocket. He pulled out a slip of purple paper and set it in one of the slots inside the cash drawer, on top of a pile of other slips of purple paper. 'I gotta put one of these in each time the register glitches like this. Y'know, to keep track of how many times it's happened.'

'Right,' I said, looking at the cash drawer full of purple paper. Then I noticed the end of Jesse's sleeves. They were stretched out and stained with black. It had to have been from how much money he handled. The bottom of my piggy bank was always caked with black dirt too.

 **Monday.**
The cafeteria.

I found Gidget and Slug sitting at a table
near the front exit. Brayden wasn't there though.
He was still probably in line getting his meal.

'How's your project coming along?' Slug
asked, shovelling a scoop of meat and gravy
into his mouth.

'There's still a lot to do,' I said. 'But I've got
plenty of time before the Bash on Friday.'

'You've got the whole thing built,' Gidget
said. 'All you really need to do is add the
finishing touches, right?'

'Right,' I said. 'Some paint and extra little things to glue onto it.'

'What is it again?' Slug asked before shovelling another huge bite of food into his mouth. He had just about cleared his tray of food in the last twenty seconds.

'It's just an entryway,' I explained. 'It'll stand in the lobby, next to the statue of Buchanan, who will hopefully find his head by then. It's going to look like you're walking into a circus

with fake robots and electronics and tubing. It's gonna be junky sci-fi stuff.'

'Sounds cool,' Gidget said. 'But why?'

'Why not?' I asked. 'Zoe's all about presentation, and I thought it'd be pretty cool if that was the first thing kids saw when walking through the doors on Friday night.'

'Makes sense,' Gidget said, but I wasn't sure if she was actually paying attention. She was back to tapping on her phone.

'So hey,' Slug said nervously. 'I was thinking…'

'Did it hurt?' Gidget asked, and then clenched her fist, whispering to herself. 'Oh, burn! Easy, Gidget, don't celebrate yet. Wait until he's begging for mercy. Only then can you gloat. That's good sportsmanship.'

For a second, I thought Slug was going to be serious… but he wasn't.

'Giraffes?' Slug said, tilting his head. 'Too tall? Or not tall enough?'

'What kind of question is that?' Gidget asked.

'The kind of question a scientist asks,' Slug

said confidently. 'How do you think scientists get so smart? It's because they ask questions.'

'But their questions aren't about giraffes being too tall,' Gidget said.

'Wait,' I said. 'Slug might be onto something here.'

'Seriously?' Gidget sighed.

'Are giraffes just horses with super long necks?' I asked, looking at Slug.

'No,' Gidget said, letting her phone drop to the table.

'And if they are, then why do *they* get the long necks?' I continued.

'Could you ride a giraffe?' Slug said.

I shrugged, looking at Gidget.

She raised her eyebrows. 'Y'know,' she said honestly. 'That's a good question. I don't think so … but … I don't know.'

'See?' Slug said, sitting back and crossing his arms. 'I'm askin' all the important questions over here.'

'Can you imagine riding an army of giraffes into battle?' Gidget said.

I tried to imagine that. 'It would either be the funniest thing ever, or the most terrifying thing ever. Either way, the army *without* the giraffes would lose.'

'Dudes,' Slug said, super seriously. He had the most intense look in his eyes. 'What if the army riding the giraffes ... was a *ninja* army?'

I laughed, imagining a bunch of ninjas riding on the backs of giraffes.

'This just in,' I said, making my best radio DJ voice. 'That idea is awesomesauce.'

'You should put robot giraffes on your entryway,' Slug suggested. 'That would be epic.'

For a moment, I seriously considered it, but then shook the idea out of my head. 'Nope,' I said. 'Besides, Brayden might get upset if I changed anything about it.'

'Why?' Gidget asked.

'Because he helped me with it over the weekend,' I said. 'Speaking of Brayden, have you guys seen him?'

As if to answer my question, Gidget gasped. A split-second later, I heard some other kids in the lunchroom do the same. Everyone was looking out of the tinted glass windows next to the table my friends and I were sitting at.

Outside in the lobby, I saw Brayden, but he wasn't alone. His head was down as he walked slowly in front of two hall monitors wearing suits that they probably didn't need to be wearing.

Following behind was Principal Davis, carrying a white object that looked familiar.

'Whaaaat?' I whispered.

'Did *Brayden* take the head?' Slug asked.

'No way,' I said. 'There's no way!'

'It's not the whole head though,' Gidget said, pressing her face against the glass wall of the cafeteria, staring out the window. 'It's just the hair. It looks like the rest broke off or something.'

Brayden stopped at the front door of the office and turned. His eyes met mine, and he shook his head with barely any movement. It was his ninja way of telling me he didn't do it. Okay, it wasn't really a *ninja* way of telling me, but that just sounds way cooler.

Principal Davis was the last to walk into the front office, shutting the door behind him. Through the frosted glass windows, I watched as the four blurry figures marched to the back section and disappeared.

'Bummer,' Slug said. 'Just when ya think ya know a guy.'

'He didn't do it,' I said. 'He *wouldn't* have done something like that. I've known him for—'

'A few months,' Gidget said, interrupting me.

I paused, nodding. 'A few months, but that's

more than enough time to get to know a guy, and I know that Brayden would never ever do a thing like this.'

Some kids walked into the cafeteria from the lobby, already in conversation.

'Someone said they saw it fall out of Brayden's book bag!'

'He's so busted, and good thing too, because that's just wrong – taking the head of a statue like that.'

'Yeah, what'd he think was gonna happen? This'll go on his permanent record, for sure.'

Gidget looked up from her phone. 'It fell out of his book bag?'

'He was set up,' I said confidently. 'That's the only answer that makes sense.'

'I don't know…' Gidget said quietly.

After seeing Brayden disappear into the front office, I had lost my appetite. Slug gladly took the rest of my food and wolfed it down.

The kids in the cafeteria were in full gossip mode and it was hard to listen. After Slug finished his *second* lunch, we headed into the lobby to get away from the noise.

 **Monday.**
The lobby.

The lobby wasn't much quieter than the
cafeteria. There were students out by the statue,
still shocked about the whole thing. I stared at
the spot on the statue where James Buchanan's
head should've been. *Was* Brayden the thief?
I didn't see him before school started that
morning, so maybe...

And then I spotted Wyatt nestled away in
the corner of the nook by the front entrance
of the school. He was on the carpet, with his
knees up, chewing on his fingernails. He kept
looking back and forth over his shoulder, like

he was afraid something was going to jump out and get him.

Of course Wyatt was out there. He *had* to have something to do with Brayden and the missing head!

I marched up to him.

'What's your game this time?' I said to Wyatt.

I'm not sure that Wyatt even noticed me. He was too busy gnawing on his fingers. The nails that I could see had been chewed down so far they were pink and raw. Sick.

Wyatt looked up at me without turning his head, moving only his eyeballs. When he noticed it was me, he jumped to his feet, and stuffed his hands into his pockets. 'What do *you* want?'

'I *said*—' but couldn't finish my sentence because Wyatt's attention snapped to his left, and then he shuffled away from me, jogging down the hall to the right.

'So that was weird,' Gidget said behind me. 'Even for Wyatt.'

It was only a few days ago that I saw Wyatt

talking to Naomi after the Spirit Week assembly. I was so sure that they would join forces to try to destroy me once and for all, but after seeing how distracted Wyatt was that morning, and how he just ran away, I was beginning to doubt they'd teamed up.

Something was off about Wyatt. Maybe he cracked after Naomi told him about the Scavengers. Maybe he was spooked because he knew they were real now?

'Hasn't Brayden been framed for something before?' Slug asked, staring at the buff statue.

'No, not really,' I said. 'Back at the beginning of the year, he got caught once trying to help, but ended up getting in trouble for that.'

'So you think you're gonna look into this prank then?' Gidget asked, using the same exact words that Zoe had, not even four hours ago.

This time, I didn't even need to think about my answer. Brayden was a friend, and he needed my help. 'Of course I am,' I said, and then faced Gidget and Slug. 'I mean, of course *we* are.'

The twins smiled at me, ready for an adventure.

Gidget and Slug went down one of the hallways, waiting for the end of lunch. I took a spot by the corner where Wyatt had been sitting to collect my thoughts.

When I first arrived to school this morning, the head of the statue was where it belonged. Even after the first bell rang, it was still there.

It wasn't until about twenty minutes into the student council meeting that someone pulled the prank – that's when Jesse burst through the door to tell Principal Davis something was wrong.

So whatever happened, happened within the first twenty minutes of the school day, when everyone was *supposed* to be in homeroom. Nobody would've been in the cafeteria yet so there wouldn't have been any witnesses, and since the front office windows were frosted glass, there was no way anyone could've seen anything from there.

I wasn't sure where Brayden was that

morning, but he should've been in homeroom like everyone else.

Of course there was always Naomi or even Victor to worry about, but if they had anything to do with the prank, they probably would've contacted me by now.

Just then, a paper aeroplane almost poked me in the eye, scaring me enough that I jumped back and let out a tiny screech.

The aeroplane darted to the floor, landing at my feet.

I glanced around, but there wasn't anyone giggling the way the kids did during breakfast when they threw their toast at me.

I noticed some writing on the inside of the aeroplane.

'Great,' I sighed, picking up the plane. I was surprised at how perfectly folded the wings were. In my entire life, I've never been able to make such a flawless paper aeroplane.

I unfolded it carefully. On the inside of the plane was a short note.

Chase Cooper,

*Victor would like to meet with you behind the
cafeteria, near the dumpsters.*
—The Scavengers

'Oh, wonderful,' I muttered sarcastically.
'More drama!'

The last time the Scavengers sent me a note,
it was on fancy stationery that looked like a
wedding invitation. The note I was holding was
a flimsy sheet of paper folded into an aeroplane.

Crumpling the plane up in my hands, I jumped to my feet and shot the ball of paper towards the nearest rubbish bin like I was playing basketball. It was an over-the-top way to throw it away, but I wanted to be sure that whoever delivered it saw I didn't care.

Too bad it missed the basket.

'*Aiiiir ball,*' I sang with a high-pitched voice as I picked it up and dropped it into the bin.

As much as I would've loved meeting Victor and dealing with the Scavengers again, which was to say I wouldn't have loved it, I had more important things to worry about – like saving Brayden from detention, suspension, or even getting expelled.

 **Tuesday.
The lobby.**

The next morning, I had my dad drop me off at school a little earlier than usual. You know I mean serious business when I wake up with enough time to actually eat breakfast at home.

The cold air was still on my clothes when I stepped through the doors of Buchanan, greeted by the headless statue.

Gidget and Slug were supposed to meet me in the lobby, but they weren't there yet. I was pretty sure Brayden would be locked away in detention for the rest of the week, and whenever he gets detention, his parents ground him from his phone, the internet, and anything else people use to communicate with the outside world.

So I was on my own in the lobby.

The white powder had been vacuumed up. I knelt closer and ran my finger along the floor, scraping the carpet to see if I could make any dust pop up.

I looked up at the neck of the statue. The top of the neck was perfectly flat, like the headless mannequins at the mall.

Leaning over the base of the statue, I reached out and tapped the foot of the bear that was next to Buchanan. The bear itself was solid rock, but the platform that held the entire statue was pretty flimsy – not like it was going to fall over, but it rocked back and forth when I nudged it.

'Well, no wonder his head fell off,' I said aloud. 'This thing's a piece of junk.'

At that moment, the front-office door slammed shut. I spun around, feeling my stomach drop, and expected a lecture from the principal. I wasn't breaking any rules, but I still felt like I had been caught doing *something*.

Instead of Principal Davis, it was Ms Chen-Jung, the school janitor, grumbling as she pulled her cart of cleaning supplies through the door. She spoke to herself with a quick, but soft voice. 'Just see if it turns up somewhere,' she said in a mocking tone. 'Like someone's just gonna take it and return it like they were *borrowing* it.'

She stopped in the middle of the hallway when she noticed I was there.

For a moment, we both stared at each other.

Finally, she snapped out of her trance. 'What?' she asked, annoyed.

I laughed nervously, turning my eyes to the floor. 'Nothing! I just…um, I just…I don't know.'

'Did *you* take it?' Ms Chen-Jung asked, glaring at me.

'The head?' I asked, pointing at the statue. 'Never! I'd never—'

'My printer!' Ms Chen-Jung said, cutting me

off. 'Davis says it'll have to wait because fixing the statue before the Bash has to come first, but my maintenance closet just got that printer over the weekend, and *already* it's been stolen! *Already!* This school! Seriously, this school!'

Ms Chen-Jung gripped the handles of her cart and pushed it down the hall. A gust of ice-cold air pushed through me. I turned around to see Gidget and Slug walking through the school doors.

'Find anything?' Gidget asked.

Slug still looked half-asleep.

Gidget nodded her head at him. 'He'll be like that until about nine. His body might be awake, but his brain is still trying to switch on.'

Slug's mouth dropped open slightly as he moaned, 'Uh-huh...'

'I only got here a little bit ago,' I said. 'There's really nothing to see. The statue doesn't have a head. The neck is smooth, so it probably came off pretty easily. And the base of the whole thing rocks back and forth.'

Gidget pushed against the base with her foot,

moving the whole thing. 'Well, duh. Of course the statue broke where it did. With a shaky bottom and a head that probably wasn't attached too well, it would be easy to knock that noggin off.'

Slug grunted a laugh. 'Shaky bottom,' he slurred with a little bit of drool collecting at the corners of his mouth.

Gidget gave her brother an annoyed look.

'Hey, guys,' Slug said slowly. 'Guys, check this out…I had this awesome idea last night…'

Gidget and I waited for Slug to continue, but he might've fallen asleep again.

Gasping, Slug's eyes opened wide, and then they fell back into the half-shut position. 'We're, like, the ninjas of the school…the good guys, right? So we're, like, here to *avenge* kids who are bullied and stuff…'

'No,' I said. 'We're *not* here to avenge kids.'

But Slug ignored what I said. That, or he didn't hear me.

'So I was thinking our ninja clan needed a name,' Slug said, as if he were sleep talking.

'We'll call ourselves the School Avengers, but shorten it to the Sc'avengers so it's easier to say.'

'Dude,' Gidget said, rubbing the bridge of her nose.

'You wanna call us the Sc'avengers.' I said, flatly. 'The Sc'avengers ... the Scavengers ... Sc'avengers. Scavengers. Dude, is this clicking at all?'

Slug nodded with a dorky smile.

'When he wakes up, he'll realise,' Gidget said.

Slug's face didn't change as he swayed back and forth.

Pulling a small notepad from my book bag, I flipped it open. 'I wrote a short list of kids who I think might've had something to do with this. We'll start with the obvious ones first, like Wyatt, Jake, Naomi, Sebastian—'

Gidget interrupted me. 'Um,' she hummed. 'You can't *start* with anyone you want to start with. That's not fair to those kids. You actually shouldn't start with *anyone*.'

'What're you talking about?' I asked. 'These are the kids who have caused trouble before and—'

'You're already looking at them like they're guilty,' Gidget explained. 'That's not fair to them. Plus, it doesn't really help our case right now. What if it *wasn't* any of those kids? Then you're just wasting time by looking in the wrong place. I mean, I know Wyatt's a bad dude, but you can't just point your finger at him and say that maybe he did it.'

'But...' I trailed off, surprised. Gidget was totally right.

And then Gidget buttered some bread of knowledge for me. 'Some people only act bad because everyone expects them to act that way. What if that's what's going on with Wyatt? Like, everyone keeps *telling* him that he's the bad guy, so he just keeps *acting* like it. What if we tried treating him like a normal dude sometime?'

'You're starting to sound like Zoe,' I said, smirking.

'She's a smart kid,' Gidget said. 'I'll take that as a compliment.'

Ms Chen-Jung poked her head up from

behind the statue. Gidget and I jumped at her sudden appearance.

'What're you kids doing?' the janitor asked, suspicious.

Gidget pointed at the statue. 'Trying to figure out what happened to the head.'

'That Brayden kid took it,' Ms Chen-Jung said. 'Everyone knows that already, so I'll ask again – what are you kids doing out here?'

'We don't think Brayden took it,' I said. 'He's our friend, and we know that he would never do something like that.'

Ms Chen-Jung studied us for a moment, and then looked at the statue of James Buchanan.

'I mean, you're out here a lot, right?' I asked.

The janitor nodded.

'Is there anything you saw that might send us in the right direction?'

Ms Chen-Jung stood silently for a moment, and then said, 'I only saw the statue after the head was stolen, so I didn't actually *see* anyone take it. But ... there *was* a girl out here ... watching me clean up the mess from the corner back there. She stayed there for a long time.'

'What'd she look like?' Gidget asked.

Ms Chen-Jung shrugged her shoulders. 'I didn't see her face, but she had black hair.'

'Great,' I said. 'There's about a billion girls here with black hair.'

Gidget huffed. 'I don't think there's a *billion*.'

'You know what I mean,' I said.

I turned towards the janitor to ask her more, but she was gone – vanished, like some kind of ninja janitor that travelled between dimensions when she— No wait, she was just down the hall.

I shut my notepad and stuffed it into my back pocket. I wanted to mention that Naomi had black hair, but after everything Gidget said about not blaming someone before any evidence, I decided not to. 'Where do we start?' I asked, stressed that the only plan I had wasn't much of a plan at all.

Gidget stretched her arm out. A phone slipped out of the sleeve, landing perfectly in the palm of her hand, like it was just another part of her body that she controlled by flexing different muscles.

'We'll start with a friend of mine,' Gidget said, typing. 'I know a kid who deals with these kinds of things.'

'You have a friend who deals with the lost heads of statues?' I asked.

Slug groaned. I *think* it was a laugh, but his body still hadn't fully woken up yet so I wasn't sure.

'No,' Gidget replied, rolling her eyes. 'My friend ... deals with this a lot. She deals with, like, investigations and stuff.'

'Does she go here?' I asked.

Gidget nodded, finishing up her text. I heard the *swoosh* sound of her message being sent.

'Cool,' I said. 'Do I know her?'

'Maybe,' Gidget replied.

'Is she a sixth grader?'

'Yes.'

'Do I have any classes with her?'

'I don't know.' Gidget paused. 'Maybe?'

'Is she short?' I asked.

'Does it matter?'

'No, but is she short?'

'Not really. She's about our height.'

'Is that who you're always texting?'

'She's *one* of the people I'm always texting, yes.'

'Does she know me?'

'Yes.'

'Really?' I felt kind of excited. 'What's she say about me?'

'Are you serious?' Gidget asked, putting a hand on her hip. 'You don't even know who we're talking about and you want to know what she says about you?'

I shrugged. 'Why not?'

Gidget's phone buzzed in her hand.

'Is it her?' I asked, hopeful. 'I'll call her the *informant*.'

Gidget read the text on her phone, leaning away from me. 'You're starting to creep me out,' she said. 'But yes, it's her, and her *name* is K-pop. Don't call her the informant.'

'But I should call her K-pop?' I asked. 'Her name is K-pop?'

'She has a thing for Korean pop music,' Gidget explained, and then she snapped a picture of me with her phone. 'The music flows through her veins like blood, so people call her K-pop.'

'Are you sending her a picture of me?' I asked, uncomfortable because I didn't even get the chance to make a dorky face.

'Mmhmm,' Gidget hummed.

'You can't just…' I trailed off. 'Is she cute?'

'Guh,' Gidget groaned, rolling her eyes.

I gestured towards Gidget's phone. 'What'd she say?'

Gidget raised her phone and read her message again before answering. 'K-pop said there's not much she, herself, can do for us, but she messaged Valentine about what's going on. She's setting up a meeting between the two of you.'

'Brody?' I said.

'Yeah, Brody,' Gidget said. Her phone buzzed again. 'You need to find him during lunch. He'll be up on the second floor, in room 801.'

'I know Brody,' I said, feeling relieved. 'Tell her to tell him I'll be there.'

Gidget jabbed her brother's arm with her fist, getting him to wake up a little more. 'C'mon, dude,' she said, heading for the kitchen. 'Let's get some brekkie in you. That ought to wake you up.'

'Later, guys,' I said. 'I'll find you after I meet with Brody.'

'You're not hungry?' Gidget asked as she guided her brother like he was some sort of sleep-walking zombie.

'I already ate,' I said.

After the twins disappeared through the doors, I took a seat on the nook, staring at the statue, hoping to see something that I missed earlier.

No luck though.

From where I was sitting, I could see the aeroplane I had thrown in the bin sitting on top of a pile of crumpled lolly wrappers and other junk. Ms Chen-Jung must not have emptied that bin yet.

All of a sudden, she appeared out of nowhere, jumping up from behind the rubbish bin, scaring me half to death.

I yelped, scooting back on the carpet in the nook. '*What* are you?' I shouted. 'How do you just appear outta nowhere?'

Ms Chen-Jung smirked at me, but didn't answer. She went about her business and pulled the bag out of the rubbish bin, and along with it, my note from the Scavengers.

I tried to hide the fact that my heart was skipping beats as Ms Chen-Jung tied off the rubbish bag and dropped it on top of her cart. After that, she continued down the hall, disappearing around the corner. At least, I *thought* she disappeared. She could've been standing right behind me for all I knew.

I started thinking about the girl that Ms Chen-Jung saw yesterday. A lot of girls at the school had black hair. *Naomi* had black hair.

I didn't know why Naomi would be involved with a prank like this, but if Naomi *was* involved, then it meant Victor was too.

And Victor wanted to meet with me. I already told him no, so if I found him now, it would be on my terms, right?

I sighed. 'Looks like I'm about to meet Victor.'

 **Tuesday.
The lunch line.**

At the front of the lunch line, I handed Jesse
my lunch money, only to have the register ring
my food up as free again.

'Still broken?' I asked.

Jesse took my money and slipped another
rectangular piece of paper into the cash drawer.
'Still broken,' he said, shaking his head in
annoyance.

The air in the kitchen normally smelled of
fried chicken (even when there wasn't chicken
frying), but that's not what my nose was
picking up. There was a hint of something

nasty, like chemicals or something. It reminded me of permanent markers.

'What's that smell?' I asked.

'Food,' Jesse replied casually.

'No,' I said. 'There's something *else* though, like marker or something…?'

'Oh,' Jesse said. 'Yeah, I think someone's working on a sign in the back. For a bake sale or something.'

'Oh, cool,' I said.

'So, hey,' he continued. 'That kid who got busted yesterday… that's your friend, right?'

'Brayden?' I asked. 'Yeah, why?'

Jesse fidgeted a bit before answering. 'Just wondering. Is he okay?'

'I think so,' I said. 'Got a week in the slammer 'cause of it.'

Jesse nodded. 'Bummer, man.'

It was nice to know that other people cared about Brayden. After paying for my food, I stepped into the cafeteria, only to be greeted by a phone in my face.

'Smile,' the girl holding the phone said.

Of all the people it could've been, it was Naomi.

I wanted to ask her right there if it was her that Ms Chen-Jung had seen, but I didn't. It wasn't just because of what Gidget had said, but I thought that if Naomi somehow *was* part of it, I didn't need her knowing I suspected anything... yet.

'Please stop,' I said, stepping around Naomi.

She followed me, holding her phone out to me. 'Come on,' she said as if we were still best friends. 'I just got this new phone, and I knew you'd want to check it out! The screen is huge, and games look amazing on it!'

I didn't say anything as I took my tray and continued walking between some lunch tables.

'Chase,' Naomi said, getting ahead of me. 'Come on...'

I had to stop walking because she cut me off. Setting my tray down on the table beside me, I gave up and took a seat. Naomi took the spot across from me, still pointing her phone at me.

'Are you recording a video?' I asked.

Naomi smiled. And then she set her phone on the table. 'Sorry,' she said. 'It's just...it's a new phone, y'know? I'm pretty obsessed with it, filming everything like crazy. I've never had a phone that shot in 1080p before, and I—'

I think she could tell I wasn't interested.

'Sorry,' she said again, softer that time. 'I've filmed so much video on this thing that it probably weighs more than your phone now.'

'That's not how digital works,' I said.

Naomi paused, and then quietly said, 'I *know*...it was a joke.'

The silence between us was awkward, so I scarfed down all my food like my life depended on it, which if you think about it, everyone's life depends on them scarfing food. Right?

'I miss you,' Naomi said flatly.

It was weird to hear her say that. I almost coughed up my food.

She must've understood my reaction because she continued, 'Not in a cheesy romance movie kind of way. I miss you as a *friend*, dork.'

I said nothing, but it was killing me.

Naomi chuckled to herself. 'Remember that time you spent the whole day talking like a caveman?'

Nāomi put on a low voice and did the worst impression of a caveman I'd ever heard. 'Oog! Chase not finish homework. Ooga, oog! Chase need bathroom! Chase go number one! Maybe number two? Chase not sure until Chase go to bathroom! Wait, teacher just want Chase to find tree?'

I couldn't help it. I cracked a smile. 'I only

did that because I lost a bet,' I said, surprised at how normal it felt to talk to Naomi. 'It was either that or wear a dress to school. When my dad wins a bet, you better be sure he makes me follow through with my end of the deal.'

'You got in-school detention because of that,' Naomi laughed.

'Just for one period,' I said. 'Mrs Olsen was pretty annoyed though.'

Naomi smiled at me, but didn't say anything else right away. I think she just wanted things to feel normal between us for another second.

'I know things can never be the same with us again,' Naomi finally said. 'But I want you to know that I'm sorry. I'm sorry about everything that happened.'

I couldn't believe my ears. Naomi was apologising for the fact that she had turned against me, and that she had turned the entire school against me. Like saying sorry was going to fix all the damage she'd done.

I really didn't feel like sitting across from her anymore because I knew that if I started flappin' my mouth, I was only going to say something I'd regret.

Besides, I still needed to get outside to see if Victor was around.

'Okay,' I said to my ex-bestie as I took my tray and got up from my spot. 'You're sorry. Got it.'

As I walked to the rubbish bin, I was afraid Naomi was following me, but when I looked over my shoulder, she was still at the table all by herself, staring at the spot where I had been sitting.

My insides crawled, but not how I thought they would. I was shocked because I wasn't happy to get away from Naomi. I was sad that she was alone.

I shook the feeling and emptied my tray into the rubbish bin.

Brody wanted me to find him during lunch, but before that, I had a couple of questions for Victor.

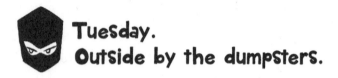 **Tuesday.**
Outside by the dumpsters.

About a minute later, I was outside.

The dumpsters were to my right. There was a small security camera pointed right at the giant dumpsters, probably to keep kids from tagging them with spray paint.

Not that anyone would ever want to hang out by the dumpsters for longer than a couple of minutes. The stench was awful!

Have you ever felt nervous about having to do something, and then you find out that you might *not* have to do that thing because of something else? Sometimes it's the best feeling

in the world. Like, I *wanted* to talk to Victor, but I was *also* freaked out by it. So if Victor *wasn't* by the dumpsters, I would've been pretty happy about it.

But as I got closer to the spot where Victor was supposed to be, I saw a kid sitting on one of those concrete parking stops behind the dumpsters. He was alone. The only other living things around were a bunch of birds.

I quickly scanned the area for other Scavengers, but was shocked to see there weren't any. Maybe the kid on the parking stop wasn't Victor after all.

Making a wide circle, I leaned over to get a better look at the kid. I'd never met Victor before so I had no idea what he looked like. All I knew was that he was an eighth grader who wore glasses.

But when I saw the front of his shirt, I knew it was him. On the left side of his chest, there was a white patch that had the name 'Victor' sewn on it with red thread.

And I was wrong about Victor being alone. He might've been the only kid out there, but he was surrounded by a dozen pigeons. They were pecking at tiny pieces of popcorn that Victor was feeding them.

Victor looked up at me, squinting because the clear sky behind me was so bright. For an eighth grader, and the leader of the Scavengers, he wasn't that scary.

His hair was slicked back and he had an earring in his left ear. He looked like a member of one of my mum's favourite boy bands from the '80s.

Victor exhaled slowly, pressing his lips together. 'Chase Cooper,' he said. 'As I live and breathe.'

'You must be Victor,' I said.

The boy nodded, but didn't stand up. He continued to lightly toss popcorn to his bird friends. 'Pigeons are so rad, aren't they? Did you know they can fly at almost a hundred miles an hour? And they might be able to see up to twenty-six miles away?'

'Um, no,' I said honestly. 'I didn't know that.'

'They help my stress levels,' Victor said. 'I feel calm when I feed them. My headaches disappear when it's just me and my birds ... such *awful* headaches.'

'Yeeeeah,' I said, not knowing what else to say.

Victor pointed his snack towards me. 'Would you like a bag of popped corn?'

'A what?' I asked. 'You mean popcorn?'

'Some people call it that,' Victor said with a snide smile. 'I prefer calling it a bag of popped corn.'

'Yeah, *that's* not weird,' I said, and then added, 'And by that, I mean it's *totes* weird. How are you allowed to be out here right now? Eighth graders have lunch at a different time than the sixth graders. Shouldn't you be in class?'

'This *is* my class,' Victor said.

'Feeding birds is your class?' I said, confused.

'It's my free period,' he explained. 'And I've chosen to sit out here and study pigeons. It's a science credit.' Victor tossed a piece of popcorn to one of the birds. 'You left me hangin' yesterday. I was out here waiting for you.'

I looked around. 'Where are the rest of your Scavengers? I thought you'd be heavily guarded since you're their leader.'

'No,' Victor said, shaking his head. 'Not

everything needs a huge scene. I just wanted to meet the kid who beat Naomi. She's my little champion, you know. I've never met anyone who showed more promise as a Scavenger. She'll go far.'

I was gonna ask him about Naomi and the statue, but what he said distracted me. 'Wait, you just wanted to *meet* me?'

'You've started a war, Chase, and I'm going to finish it,' Victor said, looking at me through his thick-rimmed glasses. 'Part of the art of war is to know yourself, and know your enemy. Well, I know myself pretty well, and based on all the information we've got about you, I know you too. But I've realised that I've never *met* you, and I think it would be a mistake to not *meet* with my enemy... before I destroy him. Do you know yourself? I mean, do you really *know* yourself?'

'I had a dream where I met my evil clone on a space station...' I stopped my dumb mouth from talking. *Why would I talk about my weird dreams?*

Victor gave me a funny look, but continued. 'Naomi really messed up your world, didn't she?'

'You have no idea,' I said.

'She's cute, right?' Victor asked. 'She just got that new phone, and she's filming everything like a little kid with a brand new toy.' He paused. 'She didn't beat you in the end though, did she? She got greedy and missed the big picture. If only she had a little more focus with you…'

'What're you talkin' about?' I asked, my blood boiling. I was beginning to think it was a mistake to find this kid. A massive, *massive* mistake.

'I'm not gonna mess with your social life, Chase. I won't even make your friends, or anyone else, hate you. I give you my *word*. I'm just going to take the thing that matters the most to you.'

I stared at Victor. 'And what's that?'

'Your ninja clan,' Victor answered coldly.

I laughed. 'You think people haven't tried that already? Naomi did a bang-up job when she took most of them from me. They all went and joined your little club of creeps!'

Victor stood up. He was short, like, super short for an eighth grader. 'Don't forget that the Scavengers know all your secrets, including your deepest, darkest struggles and fears ...'

I was silent.

'I know you've struggled with being a good leader,' Victor said confidently. 'My plan is simple – I'll take your ninja clan away from you for good, but not in the way Naomi did. No, I'm going to show your ninjas that there's no point to your clan, that there's no point to your leadership, and that you ... have no purpose.'

I hated what Victor was saying because a small part of me was afraid he was right.

'Once your ninja clan is finished,' Victor went on, 'you'll have nothing to identify with. You'll be all alone in this school – a loner with no friends. And then you can do what you've been training to do the entire time you've been here ... disappear into the shadows,' Victor paused, smiling. 'Wanna know the best part about my plan? Nobody will notice because nobody will care.'

I kept my mouth shut. This kid was so full of himself. He knew what he was going to do, and he knew there wasn't anything I could do to fight it.

'Ouch, right? Man, I'm an evil dude!' Victor said loudly, and doing the robot dance while making a beat with his mouth. *'Nnn-st, nnn-st, nnn-st, nnn-st, nnn-st, nnn-st, nnn-st, nnn-st!'*

I tried to say more, but Victor just kept doing the robot and making techno sounds every time I tried to speak. It was a little like Zoe and Faith when they were beatboxing. Was this something that was cool now? Was I late to the beatboxing party or something?

Backing away slowly, I left the kid to dance by himself by the dumpsters.

Victor was easily one of the strangest kids I'd ever met at this school. He was also one of the scariest.

 **Tuesday.
The second floor.**

Within minutes, I was on my way up the stairs
to the second floor of the school. Lunch was
almost over, and I'd already messed up twice by
speaking to Naomi and Victor. I should've just
come to Brody right at the beginning of lunch.
I probably wouldn't have felt so defeated if I had.

On the second floor, I scanned for room 801.
Most of the upstairs rooms were science labs
and storage rooms, so I wasn't sure why Brody
wanted me to find him up there.

As I passed the rooms, I could see some of
the students through the tall rectangular

windows on the doors. At this time of day, the rooms were filled with seventh and eighth graders.

I turned the corner and started down another hallway. The sunlight was hitting the ground just right, glaring off the polished floor and hitting me right in the eyes. The first floor was covered in carpet, but the second floor was one hundred per cent lino.

The hallway I was walking down was still in the 600s so I still had a way to go until I got to room 801.

I knew I'd be fine as long as there weren't hall monitors roaming the hallways. Or even worse, any of the red—

A *swoosh* came from behind me. I spun around but didn't see anything. It was completely silent, and the air was calm.

A little *too* calm.

Another *swoosh* came from the opposite direction. I spun again, but there was nothing there.

'Great,' I whispered. And then I spoke up. 'Helloooo?'

Another *swoosh*, again from behind, but this time when I turned around, I was facing a small herd of red ninjas. They were at the end of the hall, about three metres away from me. Their masks were different – still red, but with a pattern.

'Of course,' I huffed, pulling my ninja mask from the hood of my sweatshirt, and yanking it down over my face.

At that second, the ninjas started sprinting after me. I bolted.

I sprinted down the hallway, my feet hardly making a sound. All I wanted to do was get away from Wyatt's red ninjas, not alert the entire second floor that we were running around.

At the corner of the hallway, I dropped to my thigh and slid along the ground, popping back up after I cleared the turn.

COMING SOON...

THE UNTIMELY DEATH OF CHASE COOPER'S SOCIAL LIFE

NEW MASK??

YELLOW CAPE?? (TRUST ME. IT'S YELLOW)

But standing in my way was *another* red ninja. It *had* to be Wyatt because he was standing in place, watching his ninjas carry out his orders. Like the ninjas chasing me, Wyatt was wearing a new mask. He also had a yellow cape draped over his left shoulder. He must've upgraded his armour.

Suddenly, two hands grabbed at my forearms from behind, while a third hand clutched the top of my ninja mask.

The second I felt the cloth slide up on my face, I pulled my arms free. I grabbed my mask and pulled it back down before it was completely ripped off.

Wyatt was still standing a metre away. He was staring at the scuffle with his arms crossed.

Wyatt had always refused to unmask me in front of anyone – it was some kind of ninja code for him.

So why was he just standing there as his ninjas tried to take my mask off?

Again, I felt fingers slide under the back of my mask.

I dropped to the ground and rolled backwards, away from the three ninjas who were tripping over each other to get their hands on my mask.

Room 801 was only one hallway down. All I had to do was get there without being unmasked. I started running as fast as I could, not even caring that my feet were stomping on the tiles like a jackhammer.

As I passed Wyatt, he stared daggers at me, but he didn't try to stop me. Something was off about him though – his eyes looked … *different*.

Once I got to the end of the hall, I tried to drop into another controlled slide, but the floor was too slick and I dropped like a ragdoll instead.

Thankfully, a set of metal lockers tenderly

caught me – by which I mean, I slammed into the wall.

'Nailed it,' I groaned, rolling to my knees.

The sound of a door opening nearby shocked me back to reality, and I quickly sat up, pulling my mask off my face and stuffing it into the back of my hood.

Dizzy and confused, I forced an awkward smile, trying my best to hide the fact that I had just got my butt kicked by a bunch of lockers.

'Chase?' a boy asked from the door that had opened.

It was Brody Valentine.

'Dude,' he said. 'Is that you makin' all that noise out here?'

I nodded as I painfully brought myself to my

feet, grunting like an old man. I sounded like my grandpa.

'Are you trying out for gymnastics or something?' he joked.

I nodded again, trying to be funny.

Brody left the doorway and swiftly walked to the end of the hall, where the red ninjas had just been.

'Brody, wait!' I said, clutching a painful cramp in my side.

He leaned over and peeked down the hallway, but didn't act as if anything was wrong. 'What?' he asked.

I stared at him. 'Oh,' I said. 'Is there anyone there?'

'Nope,' Brody said, shaking his head. 'Was there supposed to be?'

'Uhhhhh, no,' I replied. 'I mean, like, why are you looking down there?'

'I'm just making sure none of the teachers heard you banging around like a monkey with a new drum set,' Brody said. He pointed at the room with the open door. 'After you.'

I wasn't sure where the red ninjas had hidden themselves. Being a ninja myself, I knew they had to be in one of the empty classrooms nearby ... or hiding in the ceiling tiles above us ... or even squeezed into some lockers. They were watching us, and it made me uneasy, but I had to let it slide. I was with Brody now, and there was a case to be solved.

 **Tuesday.
Room 801.**

Room 801 was dark, but I could make out
monitors mounted to the wall in front of a
keyboard and mouse.

It took a second for my eyes to adjust, but
when they did, I saw that Brody and I weren't
alone. There were three other students sitting at
a round table at the back of the room.

I lifted my hand and waved. 'Sup,' I said.

Brody let the door shut behind him. Taking
a seat on a small stool with wheels on it, he
rolled over to the screens on the wall and
tapped at the keyboard.

'Sooooo,' he said softly. 'Whassup?'

'Y'know,' I said. 'Same stuff, different day.'

'Same stuff?' Brody asked. 'What's that mean? You deal with headless statues every day? Like, is that your job?'

The kids at the back of the room laughed.

'Don't look at them,' Brody said. 'You're not allowed to look at them.'

I wasn't sure if he was joking, so I stared at the floor.

Brody laughed. 'Dude, I'm messing with you!'

Brody clicked the mouse, lighting up all the monitors at the same time. The bright screens lit up the dark room, and I was able to see the faces of the three other kids.

I knew two of them from class – Linus and Maddie. I'd never seen the other girl before. Maddie was in my English class, and she was friends with Zoe.

I knew Linus from science. He had a seat way in the back, and only showed up to class half the time. I had no idea where he was the rest of the time.

The other girl was wearing super trendy clothing, thick-rimmed glasses, and a set of huge headphones. I could hear upbeat techno music coming from the headphones.

'Hi,' she said as she pulled her headphones off. The music filled the room. 'I'm K-pop.'

'Gidget's friend!' I said, pointing at the girl. 'You like Korean pop music!'

K-pop smirked, shrugging. 'It's like you've known me all your life,' she joked.

I wasn't sure how much Gidget had told K-pop. I doubted that Gidget would've said anything about the ninja clan, but I've been wrong before.

K-pop's face stretched out a smile. 'Soooo,' she said. 'How's Faith?'

Ugh ... Gidget must've told her more than I thought. I'd had a crush on Faith since the first week of school. We weren't going out, but I wasn't sure if it was because I was too lame to officially ask her or if it was because of some other ... *better* reason?

'She's good,' I said, looking around the room,

K-POP
LINUS
MADDIE

trying my best not to make eye contact.

'Who's Faith?' Brody asked, faking a clueless look.

'Seriously?' I asked. 'Do you all know?'

'The whole school knows, dude,' Brody said. 'Who cares though? So you like a girl. Whatever, right?'

I smiled. 'Right.'

K-pop started making smooching sounds.

Even though the room was dim, I'm pretty sure everyone could tell I was blushing.

'I'm just playin' with ya,' K-pop laughed. 'You can stop being all sweaty and stuff now.'

Brody laughed. 'Seriously,' he said. 'Don't worry about K-pop. She really *is* just messing with you.' He turned to her. 'K-pop, leave him alone!'

Maddie slapped K-pop's arm with the back of her hand. 'Yeah, leave the boy alone!'

I took a breath, wiping my forehead with the sleeve of my hoodie.

'Are we allowed to be in here?' I asked Brody as I glanced at the computer screens.

Brody smirked, shooting a look back to his friends. 'I think we'll be fine.'

I turned to the kids in the back. 'I just don't wanna get detention because of this. Seems like the kind of thing where you get in so much trouble that anyone within three metres of you also gets detention.'

'It's not like that,' Linus said. 'I promise it's okay. We're all allowed in here. You can even say that we sort of own this room.'

I nodded. 'Whatever you say.'

'Good,' Linus said bluntly, but with a smile.

'Chase, are you vegan?' K-pop blurted out.

'K-pop!' Maddie said, laughing out loud. 'Manners!'

K-pop giggled and slapped the table. 'Sorry! It's just so easy when you first meet someone! You seem like a cool kid.'

That time, I laughed too. K-pop wasn't shy around new people at all, which was awesome. I wished I could be more like that. Even though she was giving me a hard time, I could tell it was in good fun.

K-pop suddenly looked serious. 'So, Chase, answer the question. Vegan or not?'

I paused. 'Um,' I said, not sure what she wanted to hear. 'I don't know exactly what a vegan is ...'

Everyone in the room stared at me. And then at the same time, they all laughed. So did I. My group of friends would definitely have a good time with these kids.

Brody spun around in his chair. 'So Gidget only told K-pop a little bit about the problem,' he said, sighing. 'Why don't you tell me the *sitch*.'

I frowned. 'Sitch?'

Brody looked down, embarrassed. 'Situation. Sorry.'

'No, it's cool,' I chuckled. I pointed at the monitors. 'Why don't you tell me about all this first? I didn't know we had cameras in the school.'

Brody looked at his friends like he wasn't sure what to say. 'Not a lot of people know about these,' he explained. 'Obviously the staff know, but only a handful of kids.'

'What?' I asked, and then joked, 'Like a bunch of secret agent kids or something?'

Brody let out a small laugh, but the others didn't. They sat perfectly still, watching me.

'So the *sitch*!' I said, changing the subject quickly. 'You guys probably already know, but the head of the James Buchanan statue was stolen yesterday.'

'It was?' Linus asked from the table.

'Yeah,' I said. 'How have you *not* heard? It's trending in the halls this week.'

Brody answered for Linus. 'We've got a million other things distracting us.'

'I heard about it,' K-pop said. 'I think Principal Davis is keeping the pieces in a box under his desk too. Kinda creepy, but whatever.'

'Why do you care who stole it?' Brody asked.

I let out a sigh. 'My friend is taking the heat for it, but he didn't do it. He's rotting away in detention right now because someone stashed it in his book bag.'

'Got it,' Brody said.

'Gidget asked if you guys could see if the video cameras caught anything,' K-pop added. 'Brody, play the video feed.'

'Right,' Brody said, tapping away at the keyboard in front of him.

The monitors all flashed as he punched in a code and moved the mouse around. Finally, he brought up the folder of videos from the day before. He clicked on a video file that was from the lobby.

'What time did it happen?' Brody asked.

'Right after homeroom started,' I said. 'Like, within the first twenty minutes.'

'Here we go,' Brody said as he clicked play.

The screens all showed the same video of an empty lobby. Nothing was happening.

Brody grew impatient and clicked fast-forward. Through squiggly lines, we all watched, waiting for someone to show up in the video.

Finally a figure appeared, walking through the lobby. Brody released the mouse and the video played at normal speed.

'There,' Brody said.

I leaned closer to the screen. The kid on the screen was pushing a cart that was covered with a white sheet. He was moving carefully through the lobby, bobbing his body back and forth, making sure nobody else was coming before moving forward and repeating the motion.

'What's on the cart?' Maddie asked.

'I don't know,' I said. 'It looks big though.'

'Can you see his face?' Linus said.

'No,' Brody answered. 'The camera angle is too high up, and he's keeping his face down whenever he looks behind him.'

And then the boy in the video pushed the cart hard, accidentally making it swerve to the left, crashing into the statue of Buchanan. As soon as he did it, the base of the statue jerked, and rocked back and forward. That's when Buchanan's head broke off from the statue's neck, crashing to the floor and cracking into three pieces.

'Boom,' Brody said. 'That's your guy.'

The boy in the video was clearly freaking out, spinning in circles. There wasn't any sound in the video, but I'm sure the head would have hit the ground loudly.

The boy scooped up the three pieces of the statue. Again, he looked back and forth, but stopped to stare down the hall. Someone must've been coming because he immediately ran to the side of the lobby with the pieces of the statue cradled in his arms.

'When do you put it in Brayden's book bag?' I whispered to myself, watching the panicked kid in the video.

What happened next confused me even more.

The boy ran to the rubbish bin next to the nook – the same one I had thrown the paper aeroplane away in.

Then he dumped the pieces of the statue *into* the bin.

'Wait,' I said. 'He didn't keep the pieces of the statue? He just tossed them? What about Brayden? How'd they end up in his book bag?'

The video feed cut out, playing static on the screen.

'What happened?' I asked, feeling frantic. 'Where'd the video go?'

Maddie, Linus and K-pop were shuffling around in the back, just as surprised as I was.

'I don't know,' Brody said, clicking the rewind button. The video scrolled back, but cut off at the same spot. 'The video just stops there.'

K-pop stood next to me, behind Brody's chair. 'Someone deleted the rest of the video,' she whispered eagerly, like it was thrilling for her.

'That's not suspicious,' Maddie said sarcastically. 'Like, *at all*.'

'Rewind it again,' Linus commanded Brody.

Brody rewound the video until Linus told him to stop. Then he paused it.

Linus pointed at the boy on the screen. 'We can't tell you *who* it is, but look at his arms.'

I squinted, studying the arms of the boy on-screen. He was wearing a long-sleeved shirt, but the cuffs were pulled up to his elbows. There was a bunch of stuff on his forearms, but I couldn't make out what it was.

'Tattoos,' Linus said. 'Whoever you're looking for has tats all over his arms.'

'Are you kidding me?' I said. 'The dude in the video is *obviously* a kid! There's no way any sixth grader has arms loaded with tattoos!'

Linus rolled his eyes. 'They could be drawn on with a pen or something.'

'Oh,' I said. 'Right.'

'Just find a dude with drawings all over his arms,' K-pop said, 'and you'll have your guy.'

'Unless he washed the drawings off,' I said. 'But that doesn't even get me my guy. That just gets me the guy who broke the statue...not the one who put it in Brayden's book bag.'

The bell rang in the hallway. The sound of students quickly filled the quiet air.

'At least it's a place to start,' Brody said, clicking the mouse again.

The picture on the screen switched to a live feed from the camera in the cafeteria. Something strange was happening near the stage, but it was difficult to see because the camera was too far away.

Linus noticed it too. 'Zoom in,' he told Brody.

Brody slid his finger up on the mouse, giving us a close-up shot of the commotion.

A crowd of students were gathered around a spot, pointing at someone. Brody zoomed the camera in a little more, and the boy at the centre of the crowd filled the screen.

It was Slug.

Two hall monitors were leading him out as Principal Davis followed with another piece of the broken statue. Slug was getting taken away for having a piece of the statue!

I didn't waste a second, running out of the room. There was barely any time before class started, but I needed to get to the cafeteria.

 **Tuesday.
The lobby.**

I ran downstairs, taking the steps two at a time. When I rounded the corner, I saw the broken statue of James Buchanan in the lobby. Gidget was standing in front of him with her arms crossed and a look on her face that said, *Don't mess with me.*

'Gidget!' I said, slowing to a stop.

She didn't say anything. She was scowling at the door to the front office.

'What happened?' I asked, waving my hand in front of her face.

'Where were you?' Gidget asked, annoyed.

'I was upstairs talking to Brody!' I said. '*You're* the one who set up that meeting!'

Gidget's angry face softened. 'Oh, yeah,' she said. 'Well, now Brayden *and* Slug have been busted with pieces of the statue.'

'How?' I asked.

Gidget shrugged her shoulders. 'I dunno,' she said. 'We were finishing up lunch when Slug opened his backpack so he could save half his cheeseburger for later when—'

'Wait,' I said. 'Slug was going to save half his cheeseburger for later? Like, in case he gets hungry in class or something?'

Gidget nodded.

'That is the most…' I said, taking a deep breath, '…*awesome* idea in the universe!'

Gidget cringed. 'Ugh… *boys*,' she said. 'Anyway, when he opened his bag, a piece of the statue fell out right in front of everyone.'

'It must've been heavy!' I said. 'How did he not know it was in there?'

'I don't know,' Gidget said. 'Someone must have snuck it in when we weren't looking.'

'That's so coconuts,' I said. 'You gotta be real sneaky to pull that off.'

'Slug will be in detention for sure,' Gidget said. 'Does that mean Brayden's free?'

'Doubt it,' I said. 'They both had part of the statue – they both could've been in on it.'

'What'd you find out with Brody?' Gidget asked.

'Not a lot,' I said. 'The video showed someone with a bunch of drawings on their arms, but after that, it cut out.'

'It cut out,' Gidget repeated.

'Yeah,' I said. 'Like someone deleted the rest of the footage.'

'Nice,' Gidget said with more than an ounce of sarcasm. 'Looks like we got a good ol' mystery on our hands.'

'That's not even the worst part,' I said. 'The kid who broke the statue threw the pieces in the bin. That means he's not the one who framed Brayden and Slug!'

'Victor?' Gidget asked.

'Maybe,' I said. 'But I don't even wanna go

there before we know for sure if he's the one behind it. The kid gives me the heebie-jeebies.'

'Alright, boss,' Gidget sighed. 'Looks like we're after a kid with drawings on his arms.'

I nodded. 'Looks like.'

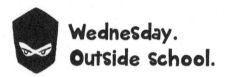 **Wednesday.
Outside school.**

I had just finished the entryway that I was building for the Buchanan Bash. I felt this sense of pride because it was one of the first things I'd ever finished that wasn't at the last second.

Pushing the door to the storage garage shut, I took a breath of ice-cold air, filling my lungs. 8:30 a.m. is early for me, so anything that helps me wake up is a good thing. I'm pretty sure I'm doomed to be a coffee addict when I grew up.

The ground even had a light dusting of

frost – the kind you couldn't see but could hear with every step taken. And at that moment, I could hear dozens of steps coming from behind the storage garage.

Being the careless kid I was, I decided to take a look.

I leaned against the outside wall of the garage as I slid down the side, keeping an eye out for anything suspicious.

And then I saw a small pack of red ninjas. They weren't running towards me, they were after another kid ... who was *also* wearing red ninja robes.

'What in the heck?' I said.

'Cooper!' the gym teacher called out from the front of the garage.

I spun around. 'Yup?'

The coach gestured towards the school building. 'If you're done out here, get back inside.'

I looked over my shoulder to see if the red ninjas were still there, but they had disappeared. 'On my way, Coach,' I said.

I couldn't make sense of what I had just seen. It *looked* like the red ninjas were chasing after one of their own, but that couldn't be possible. They had to be training or something. But training out in the open where they risked being seen? That was a new level of bold, even for Wyatt.

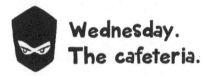 **Wednesday. The cafeteria.**

Inside the school, I met up with Gidget, and we went straight for breakfast in the cafeteria.

At the front of the line, I handed my money to Jesse. He didn't even try to make an excuse for the broken register when the food rang up for free again.

The same thing happened to Gidget when she paid.

Jesse's sleeves were still stained black, which made my stomach turn just a little as I thought about how grimy money had to be to make someone's sleeves so nasty.

Gidget and I found a table near the stage. I split open the top of my milk carton, but saw a black smear on the bottom of the waxy cardboard.

'Nasty,' I said. 'Jesse got my milk carton all filthy. I don't know if I can drink this anymore.'

Gidget inspected her drink. 'It's not on mine.'

'Lucky,' I said, setting my carton on the table.

'Slug's pretty upset about detention,' she said.

I sighed. 'So's Brayden,' I said. 'I mean, I *think* he is. I tried calling him last night, but he didn't answer.'

Gidget chucked a bit of hash brown into the air and caught it in her mouth. 'They're bummed about having to wait around while we try and figure out this whole thing, but I think they're just mad about being so bored in detention.'

'I've been there,' I said. 'Every minute feels like an hour.'

Gidget slowly chewed. She looked like she wanted to say something, but had trouble finding the words. Finally, she said, 'Slug said he's thinking about trying out for the football team.'

'That's cool,' I said.

'That would mean he'd be done with the ninja clan,' Gidget said.

I paused. 'I mean, if that's what he wants to do then he should go for it.'

Gidget took a moment, catching bit of hash brown in her mouth. 'If he leaves, I'm not sure I'll stick around either.'

I was going to say something, but Gidget spoke over me.

'It's not that your ninja clan is lame or anything,' Gidget said. 'It's just that there's not much going on in it. It's kind of...' She stopped, carefully thinking of how to put it. 'Boring?'

'Boring?' I repeated, but with hardly a sound coming from my lips.

Gidget's eyes softened. 'You're a great leader,' she said. 'Really, you are, but this whole thing just isn't what we thought it'd be.'

I was speechless. Was I losing my ninja clan again?

'It's not you,' Gidget added. 'It's me … it's us.'

'Jeez, Gidget,' I said. 'It sounds like you're breaking up with me.'

'Not with you,' she said. 'Just with the ninja clan.'

'At least I've still got Brayden,' I sighed. 'Just the two of us.'

'Yeaaaaaaaah,' Gidget said, stretching out the word. 'About that … Slug mentioned that Brayden was gonna try out for the team too.'

'Are you serious?' I asked. 'But … I mean, he never said anything to me about it!'

Gidget stared at her drink.

I couldn't believe what I was hearing. My ninja clan, *including* Brayden, the most faithful member, were all thinking of moving on.

And it wasn't like I could stop them. I didn't want to beg them to stay if they really didn't want to. If they wanted out, I had to respect that.

But I couldn't help but feel like this time was

different. It was more of a bummer for them to leave because they were bored than because they were angry.

I hated feeling like a bad leader. I thought I had moved beyond that, but there it was, staring me in the face. Maybe I just wasn't cut out to have my own ninja clan. The universe had been trying to rip it away from me since the moment I got it! Maybe it was time for me to hang up my ninja robes for good...

Victor's face flashed in my mind, and then his words floated in my head like they were on a banner that was being pulled by an aeroplane he was piloting. '... *I'm going to show your ninjas that there's no point to your clan, that there's no point to your leadership, and that you have no purpose.*'

It was a really long banner.

Scooping up my tray, I headed for the bins at the side of the cafeteria. Gidget jumped up and followed me with her tray too. She was so distracted that she left her book bag on the floor.

'Chase, wait!' she said. 'Where are you going? Would you get back here and talk to me?'

I didn't say anything as I marched towards the bins. I wasn't sure where I was going, but I knew I needed to get out of that cafeteria.

I heard Gidget groan. She stopped in the middle of the lunchroom, and headed back towards her book bag by the table.

About a second later, I heard a giant *CLUNK* echo off the walls of the cafeteria.

That was when I heard another gasp from all the students around me, along with a bunch of shocked grunts.

I turned around to see what all the fuss was about.

Gidget was back at the lunch table, standing perfectly still, with her open book bag in her hands. She was staring at the giant stone object that landed on the table in front of her.

It was another piece of broken statue.

My fingers squeezed my lunch tray. I wanted to run to her and help, but everyone in the cafeteria had already seen what happened. Gidget was the centre of attention.

She looked around the room as students shouted at her. Some of the kids were already yelling for a teacher.

Her eyes met mine, and I didn't know what to do. What was I *supposed* to do? Help her get away? Stuff the broken statue back into her book bag? Create a distraction? It was too late.

Two hall monitors wearing suits took her aside, asking her questions. She kept shrugging her shoulders and shaking her head, pointing at her book bag. I knew she wasn't getting anywhere with them because she looked frustrated as she defended herself.

Principal Davis showed up, taking the piece of statue and walking Gidget out of the cafeteria.

I was still standing in the aisle, holding my lunch tray and staring like an idiot. Gidget looked to me for help, but all I could do was watch.

Why didn't you do something? my brain screamed at me.

My knees shook as the hall monitors took Gidget through the lobby, towards the front offices. She wasn't gone yet, which meant I still had time. I could get out there and say *something. Anything!*

I jogged to the kitchen window with my tray in my hands. Without slowing down, I flipped my tray across the metal counter towards Jesse. Since I didn't finish my chocolate milk, the carton bounced right in front of Jesse, splashing milk all over him.

'Dude!' he shrieked.

'Sorry!' I yelled as I turned my jog into an all-out sprint for the front doors of the cafeteria.

Through the tinted glass walls of the lunchroom, I could see Gidget walking into the front office.

'Wait!' I barked as I burst through the cafeteria exit and into the lobby.

But I was too late. The last thing I saw was Gidget's face as she looked at me one more time before the door clicked shut.

'Crumb,' I said.

 **Wednesday.
Lunch.**

The rest of the morning went on pretty much as you'd expect at that point. Brayden, Slug and Gidget were serving out sentences in detention. Zoe and Faith were so distracted with planning the Bash that we hardly spoke.

I was going through the day on autopilot, racking my brain trying to figure out who was behind the broken statue. With everything that was happening, the only thing I could do was focus on the boy with fake tattoos. I hoped that everything would go back to normal once I found him.

I sat on one of the benches near the nook. Since it was the beginning of lunch, everyone was still in the cafeteria, leaving me with the entire lobby to myself.

The statue of James Buchanan still stood proudly, even though he was headless. 'I could really use some help now, James,' I said. 'Mr Buchanan...er...Mr President.'

I held my breath, listening carefully for him to respond.

Then I heard the sound of someone breathing. Not close, but not too far away – like maybe it was somewhere in my head.

Was James Buchanan trying to speak to me?

I sharpened my focus, listening as the quick breaths turned into footsteps scraping against the carpet.

Oh, good, it wasn't actually the president trying to contact me from the afterlife.

The footsteps grew louder until they sounded like they were right down the hallway next to the lobby.

I glanced over and saw Wyatt running at full

speed, grunting loudly as he turned the corner, disappearing again.

After that, two red ninjas appeared and disappeared the same way Wyatt had. What the heck were they running from?

And then it hit me... Wyatt wasn't running *with* his ninja clan – he was running *away* from them. They were chasing him...

'That does it,' I said. The case of the broken statue had wound me up like a ball of string, and following the red ninjas sounded like the perfect distraction.

I snuck down the side of the lobby so I was out of sight of anyone in the cafeteria. I pulled my ninja mask out of my hood and slipped it down the front of my face.

I leaned over, checking the area for Wyatt and his red ninjas. Why were they chasing after him? Were they playing some kind of weird ninja tag or something?

At the very end of the hallway, I saw the red ninjas leaning against the lockers, catching their breath and talking to each other. They kept

pointing back and forth between the two different directions in which Wyatt could've fled.

Suddenly one of the empty classroom doors next to the ninjas burst open and Wyatt jumped out, sprinting away from the two ninjas and back towards me.

'Uh-oh,' I said, pressing my body against the wall, hoping that Wyatt would run past me.

'Sup, man?' came a gruff voice from my right.

I jumped back, frightened by the kid who magically appeared. And then I jumped back again when I saw that it was another red ninja who had talked to me. And he was *big*.

The red ninja reached for the top of my mask, the same way the other red ninjas tried before.

I arched backwards, barely dodging the boy's hand, but I bumped into Wyatt as he ran past.

Wyatt grabbed the back of my hoodie and pulled me away from the big red ninja. Spinning around, I righted myself and bounced into a sprint right next to him.

'*What* are you doing?' Wyatt squawked angrily as we ran.

'What are *you* doing?' I asked, my voice muffled through my ninja mask.

'None of your business!' Wyatt said. 'Why are you even out here?'

'That's none of *your* business!' I said.

It was a pretty childish argument to have while running away from some ninjas.

At the end of the hallway, Wyatt took a hard left turn. I was going so fast that I had to throw my foot against one of the lockers to keep myself from crashing into it. For about half a second, it was like I was one of those ninjas who could run on the sides of buildings. It was pretty sweet.

The red ninjas turned the corner right behind us and continued their chase.

'*What is this? What's happening?*' I shouted.

Wyatt turned down another hall. He grabbed my hoodie again just as I was about to run past him and pulled me into another classroom.

We pressed our backs against the wall, staying out of sight as the ninjas in the hallway bolted past the door.

The red ninjas couldn't have been that smart. How could they lose the kids they were chasing and *not* check inside the empty classrooms in the hall?

Oh, probably because the classroom was full of students.

My stomach dropped.

'Whoops,' I mumbled.

Wyatt chuckled.

'Can I help you two?' the teacher asked, confused.

In front of the wide-eyed students, I moved in slow motion back to the door. Like, maybe if I moved slowly enough, they wouldn't see me. But it just made things worse. It was the most awkward thirty seconds of my life, and trust me, I've been in *thousands* of awkward situations. This was just plain embarrassing.

Once we were back in the hallway, Wyatt shut the classroom door behind us.

He glared at me and started walking towards the lobby.

'Wait!' I said, pulling my mask off. 'What the *junk* was that all about?'

Wyatt stopped, putting his hands on his hips. 'Like I said, it's none of your business.'

'Did you just *save* me back there?' I asked. 'Did you just pull me aside so your red ninjas wouldn't get me?'

Wyatt huffed but didn't answer. He was hiding something.

'Awwww,' I sang. 'Even though you hate me, you still care enough to protect me. How sweet.'

'Knock it off,' Wyatt sneered.

'Then tell me what's up!' I demanded.

Wyatt paused. His jaw muscles created small waves in his cheeks as he ground his teeth. Finally, he said, 'I'm having some...trouble with my ninja clan, alright?'

'Oh?' I said, feeling delight deep in my body, around my stomach, I think.

Wyatt snarled, clearly upset. 'I *might* have made a mistake by trying to make a ninja clan the size of a small army. And now my ninjas *might* be a little bit out of control. Jeez, and *after* I got everyone cool new ninja masks! The high-tech ones too, with the fabric that keeps your skin cool when you sweat! It's like astronaut fabric!'

'Out of control?' I asked. 'What's that mean?'

'Just don't be surprised if you see another clan pop up soon,' Wyatt muttered. His anger disappeared, melting into a worried expression.

'*Another* clan?' I repeated. 'Are you kidding me right now?'

'I wish! I can honestly say I never saw this coming,' Wyatt blurted out.

'Why were your red ninjas chasing after you?' I questioned.

'The new ninja clan *might* be looking for a new leader,' Wyatt said reluctantly. 'And the way to become the leader would be to steal my ninja mask ... or *yours*.'

I gasped. '*That's* why those guys kept trying to pull my mask off! Why in the heck would you give that order? Why would you tell them to steal *your* mask?'

'Maybe 'cause I didn't give the order, Chase!' Wyatt growled.

'But if you didn't give the order, then...' I trailed off, confused. 'Wait, are you still the leader of your red ninjas?'

Wyatt's face scrunched up so hard that I thought a black hole had formed in the middle of his brain and was pulling him in. He didn't answer. Instead, he threw his arms in the air, made a 'bah!' sound, and stormed off.

I didn't follow him. I was floored. Wyatt had been working for months on his red ninja clan, building it and recruiting half the school for it. And now he was telling me he'd lost control of it? Man, I wasn't looking forward to meeting the kid who took it from Wyatt.

Buchanan was a rough school sometimes, but from what Wyatt had said, it sounded like things were about to get much worse.

 **Thursday.
Before school.**

When I got to school the next morning, I went straight for the storage garage down by the track. I wanted to check on my project for the Bash.

The entryway I had built was finished and stored in the garage, but I had a nagging thought that either the Scavengers *or* the red ninjas would try to mess with it. I was happy to see it was still safe and sound.

I shut the garage door behind me and jiggled the handle, making sure it was completely closed.

'Everything cool in there?' a voice behind me said.

It was Victor.

I tried to hide the fact that he startled me when I turned to face him.

'Everything's fine,' I said.

'Good,' Victor said, not actually caring. 'Sooooo...' he sang as if we were old buddies. 'What's new with you?'

I stared at the leader of the Scavengers. 'You know exactly what's new with me,' I said. 'You're going around framing my friends for breaking the statue!'

Victor looked offended. '*Whaaaaaat?*' he said. 'I would *never!*'

'Whatever. I know it's you.'

'I don't know, man,' he said, shrugging. 'That's a pretty bold accusation. Do you have any proof?'

Victor knew I had nothing on him. 'No,' I said. 'Not yet, but I will...somehow.'

'Won't happen,' Victor sighed.

'What do you want?' I asked impatiently.

'I just wanted to see how you were doing this week,' Victor answered with a sly smile. 'I know you're going through a lot, and I just thought that, y'know, maybe you needed a friend or something.'

I didn't say anything. I didn't even *want* to.

Victor burst out laughing. 'I'm sorry,' he said with a hand over his chest. 'I can't keep a straight face anymore. No, hey, honestly, I just wanted to see what a mess you were in person, that's all.'

What the heck? Who does that? Who goes to the person they're picking on just to see the look on their face?

Victor leaned to the side to get a better look at the storage garage door. 'What've you got in there?'

'Nothing,' I said quickly. I didn't want Victor to know about the entryway. 'I was just, um ... practising some ... dance moves ...'

Nailed it.

'Dance moves, huh?' Victor asked. 'Whatever, dude.'

From the look on his face, I could tell he totally bought it. I stepped around the leader of the Scavengers, ending our conversation.

As I walked towards the school, I expected Victor to shout at me, the same way Wyatt did whenever I turned my back on him, but Victor didn't. He was different from Wyatt, and that terrified me.

My phone vibrated in my front pocket. I unlocked it and saw one unread message from Brody Valentine.

Not sure when you'll get 2 school, but if u have time, I'm in the library. Find me. It's important.

Pushing my phone back into my pocket, I felt a chill run all the way to my toes. Hopefully Brody had good news. I really needed some good news.

I turned to look back at the garage, to see if Victor was still there, but he wasn't. He was gone.

Five minutes later, I was in the library, keeping an eye out for any library zombies that might've been in there. You know the type – kids who hang out in the library to study, but instead text their friends, obsess over their online profiles, and watch videos of kittens so adorable it turns their brains to mush.

Luckily for me, it was too early for library zombies. The library was mostly empty, except for the librarian and a few teachers sipping coffee and reading news on their laptops.

Brody was the only student in the library, sitting at a gigantic table by himself, studying a bunch of photos spread out in front of him.

'Valentine,' I said menacingly.

'Cooper,' Brody replied. He tried spinning his chair like an evil villain, but the chair didn't spin. Instead, he just gripped the sides and leaned his body far enough that the chair bobbed back and forth until finally facing me. Instead of looking like a villain, he looked like a bobble-head.

'Whassup?' I asked, taking a seat across from him.

'Good news!' Brody said with a smile, but then his smile turned into a frown. 'Then bad news, and then I think even worse news...'

'Nice,' I sighed.

Brody slid a stack of photos across the table to me. 'After we found out that part of the security video had been deleted, I searched a bunch of other video feeds to see if any other cameras saw anything.'

I pulled the photos closer. They were screenshots from another video he must've

found. The timestamp in the corner showed that each photo was about three seconds apart. The one on top was of the empty lobby, *after* the kid with the fake tattoos had broken the statue.

'Those are from a camera further down the hall,' Brody explained. 'The video is zoomed in, but it's still too far away to see the kid's face, but... there's more.'

I flipped through the stack of photos, watching the kid with the fake tattoos pick up the pieces of the broken statue and toss them into the rubbish bin.

After that, he took his cart and wheeled it away in the opposite direction.

The timestamp said that it was about a minute later when *another* student showed up in the lobby, and headed straight towards the rubbish bin. It was like he knew exactly what was in there.

The kid was covered in shadow, which made it hard to see his face.

'Who is that?' I asked Brody.

Brody scratched his eyebrow. 'Keep going,' he said softly.

I flipped each photo over, watching the screenshots play out like a glitchy movie.

The boy reached into the rubbish bin, bending in half so he could grab it from the bottom. Then he pulled out the three pieces, carefully pushing them so that they fit where they belonged.

After that, he stuffed the statue's head into his book bag, zipped it up, and walked down the hallway, towards the camera that was filming him.

The shadows on his face crept upwards as he got closer and closer until finally, I could see who it was...

It was Brayden.

Brayden took the statue from the rubbish bin.

'I'm sorry,' Brody said.

'I don't understand,' I whispered.

'I don't either,' Brody said. 'But keep going.'

Glancing up, I spoke in a hushed whisper. 'There's more?'

Brody nodded.

I kept flipping through the photos. The camera had changed from one inside the school to one outside by the dumpsters.

'No, dude,' I said, remembering the camera I had seen when I went to visit Victor.

The printed photos continued to show me what I didn't want to see. Brayden walked out of the cafeteria doors, looking around to make sure he was alone. Then he stopped about a metre and a half away from the dumpsters.

That's when a girl walked out to meet him. It was Naomi. She was holding her new phone in front of her. Victor soon appeared further back. Brayden took two pieces of the statue out of his book bag. In the last photo, handed them to Naomi. *He handed them to Naomi!*

'Victor and Naomi are dangerous kids,' Brody said. 'And Brayden is right there talking to them.'

'I don't know what I'm looking at,' I said. 'What happened?'

Brody shrugged his shoulders. 'It looks like your buddy is playing along with Naomi and

Victor. Did you notice that Brayden kept one
of the broken pieces in his bag?'

'What do you know about Victor?' I asked.

'Nothing,' Brody said, shaking his head. 'Just
that he's a bad apple. That's what Linus and
Maddie told me, but they didn't tell me why.
They said I need to stay away from him and
from Naomi.'

I nodded. 'They're right.' It wasn't my place
to tell Brody what was going on. He had
helped me out enough, and the less he knew
about the Scavengers, the better.

Sinking in my chair, I exhaled slowly, afraid that I was going to pass out.

Brody took the stack of photos and stuffed them into his book bag. He apologised again, and headed out of the library.

I couldn't believe how everything had flipped around. Victor hardly did anything at all, but I felt like he had won. I felt like the Scavengers had won. His revenge wasn't loud or explosive. It was far worse – subtle and totally destructive.

I wasn't a good leader, and he proved that by taking my ninjas away, one by one until I was alone. But the worst part was that he got *Brayden* on his team.

I thought if there was anyone who had my back no matter what, it was Brayden. I guess I was wrong.

There it was ... the last nail in my coffin. I was done. I couldn't see any point in fighting after that. Without my friends, there wasn't any reason. The Scavengers had won, and they barely even tried.

 **Thursday.
The cafeteria.**

I sat in the library, stewing in self-pity, for a few minutes before deciding to take my little party to the cafeteria. Plus, I felt awkward being all alone in the middle of the library.

The cafeteria was better, but not by much. I claimed a table in the corner and watched kids stuff their faces with cinnamon rolls and sausages. I *wished* I could eat breakfast in blissful ignorance too.

A few minutes before breakfast was over, Jesse roped off the breakfast queue so nobody else could get in. Then he turned around and

gave me one of the most evil-eyed stares I had
ever seen. It was so angry that I could sense it
from all the way across the cafeteria.

Wonderful. Someone *else* was upset with me.
What more was this week going to bring?

Jesse stomped across to my table. His sleeves
were still stained with black grime. Punching
his angry fists down, he shouted, 'You soaked
me with chocolate milk yesterday!'

I shook my head, baffled. 'What are you
talking about? No, I didn't!'

'Yes, you did!' Jesse said. 'Right before you ran out of the cafeteria, you threw your tray at me!'

'Oh, right,' I said, remembering that I had rushed to get to Gidget before she went into the principal's office. 'Sorry, dude, it was an accident.'

But Jesse wasn't listening. 'I can't believe you just wasted that whole carton of chocolate milk! You hardly took a sip! Get a drink of water from the fountain if all you want is a sip!'

Something in me snapped and I just wanted him to leave me alone. 'I didn't drink it because you left grimy money dirt all over the bottom of the carton!' I said louder than I had meant to. 'Look at your sleeves, dude! They're caked with dirt! At least pull them up when you're working the register!'

Jesse looked at me like I was stupid. And then he pulled both sleeves up on his forearms, realising what I was upset about. 'Sorry, man,' he said, his tone changing instantly. 'These smears aren't from dirty money. Sometimes

I get bored and doodle on my arms. My mum *hates* it because all my clothes are gross with ink.'

I stared at Jesse's forearms. He had drawn on every centimetre of them. Little smiley faces, stars and skulls were sprawled across the canvas of his skin.

I sat there silently as the whole cafeteria stared at Jesse and me.

Even Principal Davis was walking towards us, probably because he heard me shouting and wanted to make sure there wasn't any trouble.

Jesse stood at the foot of my table, trying to apologise for the marker smudge on the bottom of my milk. And I was frozen because I knew I had just caught the kid who broke the head off the statue that was in the lobby. He was the mystery student with the fake tats on his arms.

'Uhhhh,' Jesse said. 'Hello?'

'*You* broke the head off the statue,' I said, my voice shaking.

Jesse's face went white. He let out a laugh. 'What?' he said. '*What are you ta—*'

'*You* broke the head off the statue!' I said louder.

Jesse coughed out a guilty laugh. 'That's crazy! You're crazy!'

'I saw you in the video!' I said. 'You bumped into it with your cart and the head fell off! And then you dumped the pieces in the bin! What was under the sheet? What was in your cart?'

Jesse forced out another laugh, but he didn't look happy.

'What's this all about?' Principal Davis asked, standing next to us.

I looked at Jesse, who was sweating like crazy. And then I looked at Principal Davis.

Jesse looked at me, and then at Principal Davis, and then back to me.

Nobody said a word.

Finally, Jesse spun around, sprinting away, but it wasn't far. The cafeteria table behind him did a pretty good job of stopping him in his tracks.

Jesse dropped to the ground, moaning in pain as he held his arms around his stomach.

'Son, are you alright?' Principal Davis asked as he helped Jesse to his feet.

Jesse's eye caught mine again. I pressed my lips together and shook my head.

The guilt must have been too much for him.

'Fine!' he roared. 'I did it, alright? I broke the head off the statue! It was me, okay? You happy now?'

Principal Davis furrowed his brow, shocked.

I was just as surprised that Jesse was confessing.

'But it was an accident!' Jesse said. 'I swear! I didn't mean to break it!'

Principal Davis was staring straight ahead, trying to make sense of the situation. '*What* are you talking about?'

'The head of the statue!' Jesse said. 'I broke it off when I bumped into it wheeling that stupid printer around!'

Suddenly, a woman screeched from across the room. 'My printer! You stole the printer from the maintenance closet! You little thief!' Ms Chen-Jung howled, running across the cafeteria.

Principal Davis put his hand up to calm her. 'Slow down, Ms Chen-Jung,' he said. 'Give him some room to talk.'

Jesse paused, sitting on top of the table. The cafeteria was silent. 'I nailed the statue with the printer.'

'The *stolen* printer!' Ms Chen-Jung said harshly.

'I borrowed it!' Jesse said defensively.

'What for?' Ms Chen-Jung asked.

'To print free-lunch vouchers,' Jesse admitted.

Principal Davis scratched his head. 'Why would you print those?'

'Because the registers have been broken all week,' I said, speaking for Jesse.

'No,' Jesse said. 'I just said that to keep people from asking too many questions. I've been...I've been ringing everyone's lunch up as free, and then pocketing the money. I used the printer to print those free-lunch vouchers so I wouldn't get caught.'

The principal shook his head.

Jesse covered his face. 'I can't do it anymore,'

he said. 'I only wanted eighty bucks for a new skateboard! Honestly, eighty bucks and that was it! But I never counted the money until about halfway through the week! I thought, y'know, it would take a while to get eighty bucks, but after the third day, I counted up all the money, and...'

'And how much was it?' Principal Davis asked.

'*Six thousand dollars!*' Jesse said, burying his face deeper in his hands.

Half the kids in the cafeteria gasped, shocked.

Jesse went on. 'I feel *terrible* about it. And for those guys who are in detention because the pieces kept falling out of their backpacks! I just... I just... I'm sorry.'

I couldn't say I didn't feel bad for the kid. He might've stolen a ton of money, but it was obvious he was torn up about it.

Even Ms Chen-Jung felt sorry for him. She awkwardly patted his shoulder. 'There, there, human child.'

Principal Davis walked Jesse out of the

cafeteria. Anything else he wanted to say would have to wait until he was in the principal's office with his parents.

I sat back down and took a deep breath, wondering why the heck I didn't feel any better.

I'd finally figured out who was behind the cracked statue, which meant that my friends would be out of detention within the hour. That should've been great news!

But then I remembered the screenshots from the security cameras. Brayden was free from detention, but now I knew he was working with the Scavengers. And sooner or later, I'd have to ask him why.

 **Thursday. Lunch.**

I wasn't surprised to see a new face behind the register during lunch. Her name tag said 'Beatrice'. She took my lunch money and placed a mini cupcake on my tray. 'Thank you,' she said.

'Um,' I said, staring at the tiny cupcake. 'What's the deal with the small baked item?'

'Oh,' Beatrice said, smiling. 'I'm part of Cupcake Kids. We're a club for kids – we take classes, and go on trips and stuff. We'll be having a bake sale in a few weeks, and these cupcakes are a sample of what we'll have there.'

I stared at the cupcake on my tray. 'Huh,' I grunted. 'I've never heard of Cupcake Kids before.'

Beatrice smiled wider. 'We're pretty new,' she said. 'I'm sure you'll hear more about us soon.'

'Thanks for the cupcake,' I said.

'No,' Beatrice said. 'Thank *you*.'

Before picking my tray up from the conveyor belt, I asked, 'Do you know what happened to Jesse?'

'His fate is in the hands of the school now,' Beatrice said sadly. But then she added, 'Just kidding. As long as he returns every dollar he stole, he'll only get suspended for a week.'

'Oh, good,' I said, relieved.

I was happy to hear that Jesse was gonna be alright. Suspension is pretty bad, but it could've been *much* worse for him. Six thousand dollars isn't exactly a small amount of money. If he had *kept* it, Jesse could've been nailed with juvie.

I scanned the cafeteria for a place to sit. There was an empty table right in the middle. It wouldn't have been my first choice, but since it was my only one, I made my way down the aisle.

Brayden, Gidget and Slug were nowhere to be seen, which was good news for me. My brain was still spinning because of the photos Brody showed me in the library. If I had to talk to Brayden right now, I wasn't sure what I'd say.

Finally, I set my tray down on the empty table. At almost the same instant, a kid sat at the other side of the table, across from me.

It was Naomi.

I sighed, leaning my head against my hand, jabbing at my food with my fork. I was too drained to care.

Naomi took her phone from her pocket and started filming me again.

'Seriously?' I said. 'Give it a rest.'

Naomi's mouth tightened into an embarrassed smile. 'Sorry,' she said, setting her phone face-up on the table. 'I'm just so pumped about this phone.'

'I can tell,' I said.

'Don't take it personally,' Naomi said, lifting

her book bag and setting it next to her lunch tray. Something inside made a *CLINK* sound. 'I've been filming everything.'

'Riiiight,' I said. 'Because you're a Scavenger, and Scavengers spy on everyone everywhere.'

Naomi didn't say anything. She unzipped her bag and reached in, fishing around for something.

I took the cupcake that Beatrice had given me, and popped the whole thing into my mouth. 'Mmm,' I said with cheeks full of dry cupcake. 'These are *not* good. How was yours?'

'I'd love to tell you it was totes sweet, but I guess I wouldn't know,' Naomi said, and then arched her neck so she was looking back at the kitchen. '*Would I, Beatrice?*'

'She forgot to give you one?' I asked.

'Right.' Naomi said. '*Forgot.*'

'Why are you sitting with me?'

Naomi blinked, like she was trying to think of a good way to answer. 'I don't know,' she said honestly. 'The past week or so has been tough on me.'

I laughed. 'Tough on *you*? What about *me*? What about everything that's happened to *me* since learning about your little club of creepy spies?'

'I know,' Naomi murmured. 'I guess I just want things to feel normal.'

'What's normal?' I asked, setting my fork down.

'Sitting with you during lunch,' Naomi said. 'Talking about *nothing*. Giving each other a hard time.'

I pushed my tray to the side, and let my

head drop on the table. My forehead thunked hard enough that Naomi's book bag made another *CLINK* sound.

It didn't surprise me that she and Victor were the ones behind framing the kids from my ninja clan. But it was because of Brayden that I felt so defeated. I was numb, and I didn't even care that Naomi was trying to speak to me.

I just gave in.

Naomi reached into her book bag again, and pulled out a small teacup. She set it gently next to her lunch tray and ran her fingers against the rim.

There wasn't anything special about the teacup. In fact, it looked like it had been broken at one time. All along the sides of the cup were cracks that had been filled with gold-coloured sparkly glue.

'Nice cup,' I said. 'Do you bring your own salad dressing to school too?'

Naomi didn't pick up my joke. 'No,' she said, pouring her juice into the teacup.

I raised my head, watching her carefully pour

her drink. 'What is this? I've never seen you do this before.'

'I only started doing it about a week ago,' Naomi said. 'It helps remind me of who I am.'

I chuckled nervously because I had no idea what she was talking about. She sipped at the teacup, keeping her little finger out. It was bold. Kids would make fun of her if they saw her – a sixth grader playing tea party in the middle of the cafeteria? That was social death. But Naomi didn't give a rip about what other kids thought of her.

Every molecule in my body wanted to be angry with her. She had betrayed me. She had made half the school hate me. She took my ninja clan away from me. But I just couldn't, at least, not at that moment in the cafeteria.

So I gave in, and acted like she was an old friend. I have to admit, it was easier than I thought it would be.

'Naomi,' I said. 'I'm really struggling this week.'

'I know,' she said, sipping from her cup. 'I

used to be in your
ninja clan. I know
how poorly you
deal with stress.'

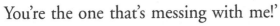

I couldn't help but
laugh. 'Some of the
stress is from you though!
You're the one that's messing with me!'

Naomi shook her head. 'It's Victor this time,'
she said. 'Not me.'

'I know that Brayden went to you with the
broken pieces of the statue,' I said. 'I know you
were there with Victor.'

Naomi didn't say anything.

'You're probably the one putting those statue
pieces in everyone's book bags too, huh?' I said,
hoping I was wrong.

Naomi leaned forward. 'It *wasn't* me.'

'Then who?' I asked.

Naomi shrugged her shoulders. 'Could've
been anyone,' she said. 'There are Scavengers
around this whole school. They're probably
even listening to us right now.'

I rolled my tongue in my mouth, peeking out of the corner of my eye to see if anyone was staring. Nobody was.

'Why did Brayden do it?' I asked.

Again, Naomi shrugged her shoulders. 'I don't know. He just showed up with the pieces from the statue. I bounced before Victor and Brayden talked.'

I shook my head. 'I don't know what to do anymore,' I said.

'What do you mean?' Naomi asked, pouring more juice into her teacup.

'This whole year has been one huge struggle,' I said. 'It's like this school wants to crush my spirit, but I've refused to give in … until now.'

Naomi set her teacup down. 'Why now?'

'Because,' I said, 'I was too thick to see that I was fighting a losing battle. Wyatt, the red ninjas, the Scavengers, you … all of you have pushed me, and I just kept pushing back.'

Running her finger along the rim of her teacup, Naomi said nothing.

It was like I had opened the door to my

thoughts and I couldn't get it shut again. 'I've worked so hard to be a good leader – even Victor knew it, which was what he was trying to take from me this week. Well, it looks like he won. He did it, and without lifting a finger. If I was any good at being what I wanted to be, then it shouldn't have been so easy for him to win.'

'I know,' Naomi said softly. She sounded really sad.

'Victor has shown me who I really am,' I said. 'And I know that was his point. I was already on the edge. All he needed to do was nudge me.'

'Aren't we all on the edge though?' Naomi asked.

'No?' I said. 'I dunno, maybe? I'm just… I'm so tired, Naomi. I'm so tired of trying to be strong all the time. My ninja clan looked to me for leadership. My friends counted on me to be there when something went wrong. Everyone expects me to know what I'm doing!'

'I think everyone feels that way,' Naomi said, smiling slightly.

And then I finally found exactly what I was trying to say. 'I just want someone to tell me that it's okay to struggle. That I'm *allowed* to! That it's okay to not be strong all the time!'

Naomi stared at me with eyes as big as the rings of Saturn. I was beginning to worry that maybe I had said too much, and now her brain was sizzling to a crisp.

I opened my carton of milk and took a swig. 'Sometimes I just wish I had never started my ninja clan. Life would be a lot easier.'

'I'm only going to say this once to you,' Naomi said. 'Because I can't give life advice to anyone without feeling like I'm in a cheesy movie about growing up... but it *is* okay to struggle. You're allowed to. We're *all* allowed to.'

I looked at Naomi.

'Your biggest fight has been with yourself,' Naomi said. 'You've tried to be perfect, and I have to give it you, you've done a good job of getting close to it.'

I wasn't sure what to say. I was already starting to feel embarrassed.

Naomi leaned back in her chair. 'But you know what? None of that matters, does it? Does your ninja clan really matter?'

'Yes,' I said. 'No? I'm not sure how you want me to answer that.'

'Your ninja clan,' Naomi explained. 'Even though it's important to you, and will always be important, doesn't really matter in the end.'

I stared at Naomi's smiling face, confused. 'Huh?'

'The ninja clan isn't special,' Naomi said. 'It's the people in it who are ... Your *friends*. I haven't missed the *ninja clan*. I've missed being *friends* with you.'

I shrugged. I wasn't sure why I still wanted to argue. 'Still feels like I've failed.'

'It's cool,' Naomi said, leaning forward. Her eyes sparkled. 'Everyone fails. You're allowed to fail, Chase. You're allowed to struggle.' She took her teacup in her hand and raised it towards me.

'No thanks,' I said. 'I have my own drink.'

'No, ya dingus,' Naomi said, wagging the

teacup at me. 'I don't want to you drink it. I want you to look at it.'

I stared at the cup in her hand. 'Okay? It's an old, cracked teacup. So?'

'*Kintsugi*,' she said.

'Kint-wha?' I replied.

Naomi admired the teacup, running her fingers along the cracks. 'I broke this cup when I was, like, three. My dad glued it back together with some sparkly glue, and then explained what *kintsugi* is.'

'Sounds Japanese,' I said.

'It is,' Naomi said. 'You know my dad is Japanese, right?'

'Yeah, of course,' I said, lying through my teeth.

Naomi continued. '*Kintsugi* means "golden joinery". It's the art of repairing broken pottery with gold lacquer. Well, in this case, gold sparkly glue.'

I studied the cracks in the teacup. The sparkles caught the light, glimmering like tiny diamonds.

Naomi continued. 'It's the idea that this cup is more beautiful because it's been broken.'

'But you could've just used white glue,' I said. 'And hidden the fact that the cup was ever broken at all.'

'That's not the point,' Naomi said. 'The gold makes the cracks obvious because that's what's special about the teacup. We don't want to hide the fact that it broke... that it struggled... because that's an important part of the teacup's story.' She turned the cup slowly in her hand. 'No other cup will ever look like *this* cup.'

'That's why you've been using it this week?' I asked.

Naomi paused. 'I've always kept it in my bag,' she said. 'I've just never used it before. I've made a lot of mistakes. Being a Scavenger was one of them. Hurting you was another.'

I stared at the table. This was one of the heaviest conversations I'd ever had at this school, and I've had a couple of doozies.

Everything that Naomi said about my ninja clan was spot on. It was important to me, and being a leader was just as important, but none of that even came close to how important my friends were.

Without my friends, what was the point? What was the point of ninja training? What was the point in figuring out the mysteries?

I had warm fuzzies from the light bulb that had switched on.

The whole reason I was having a pity party in the first place was because Victor had won. He won by taking away my ninja clan, but it didn't matter. None of my friends were going to turn their backs on me, because I didn't have a ninja clan anymore.

I didn't need to be their leader, I needed to be their friend.

I felt a surge of energy in my veins. It felt good. Probably the same way a robot feels when their battery is fully charged.

My friends were the most important thing to me, and Victor couldn't take *that* away.

Victor's grip, even the Scavengers' grip, on me was gone.

I opened my mouth to say more to Naomi, but she had disappeared. I quickly scanned the cafeteria, but she was gone.

The only thing left was a slip of paper on the table in front of me. I unfolded the paper and read it.

You should probably check the principal's office for the three pieces of the statue. Davis has been keeping them in a box under his desk.

It wasn't signed, but I knew Naomi's handwriting anywhere. I couldn't tell if she was warning me, or just giving me a heads up.

All I had to do was peek into the principal's office and check the box right under his desk.

No big deal, right?

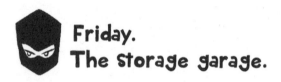 **Friday.**
The storage garage.

I had my dad drop me off right by the storage garage before school. I still hadn't spoken to Brayden, and I risked running into him if I went *through* the school building.

I opened the side door to the garage and stepped inside, feeling the hot air hit my face.

The project I had worked so hard on was standing tall in the middle of the garage. It loomed over two-and-a-half metres high, and was built to look like the entrance to a cool robot carnival. I hoped Zoe would dig it.

Thankfully, my project was still untouched.

It would've been easy for any of the Scavengers or even the red ninjas to have found their way into the garage to destroy it.

At the top of the entryway was a sign that I had made out of aluminium foil.

After making sure everything was in order, I took a white sheet and threw it over the top of my project so that it would be hidden when it was in the cafeteria. Principal Davis wanted to unveil it at assembly in the cafeteria that morning.

Zoe had arranged for the whole school to skip homeroom so everyone could be at the assembly. She even had a local cafe come and set up a breakfast buffet.

I pulled my phone out of my pocket and a slip of paper fell to the floor at my feet.

It was the note that Naomi had left on the table the day before. The one that told me I should check Principal Davis's office.

I checked the time on my phone. There was still thirty minutes until school started, and over an hour before the assembly. Did I have time to take a peek inside the principal's office? Of course I did.

 **Friday.
The cafeteria.**

I ran back to the cafeteria doors. To the left of
the cafeteria doors was another entrance that
led behind the stage.

I ducked down so nobody eating breakfast
would spot me. The windows went all the way
down the side of the cafeteria. If I wanted to
get to the backstage door, I had to get past the
windows.

Taking my ninja mask from my hood, I
slipped it over my face in the cold weather.
Puffs of steam filtered through the black cloth
of my mask, drifting up in front of my eyes.

Staying crouched, I waddled like a duck, until I was a safe distance from anyone in the cafeteria. I rolled to my feet and ran through the backstage door.

The warm air was thick and swampy. *Sick.*

The principal's office wasn't far. The cafeteria, lobby, and front-office counter were the only things standing in my way. It wasn't going to be easy, but nothing ever was for a ninja.

And then it struck me... why was I running around with a ninja mask? I could just walk over to the front office, and *then* slip on my mask if I needed to.

I shook my head, pulling my ninja mask off my face. 'Dummy.'

At the side of the stage, I pulled the red velvet curtain back and jumped to the floor of the lunchroom. There were hardly any students in there except for Zoe and Faith, along with the crew that was going to dish out the breakfast buffet.

'Chase?' Zoe asked from across the room. 'Um, what're you doing on the stage? Wait, don't answer that. I'm sure it's ninja stuff, and I'm not in the mood to stress out over whatever you're doing. You can tell me after all this is over.'

I laughed. 'You got it.'

Faith ran to my side and held her phone out. 'Smile,' she said, snapping a selfie of us. Then she turned and said, 'Where the heck have you been all week? It's like you've been a total loner or something.'

'Kind of,' I said, nodding. 'It's been pretty crazy... I mean, boring. A pretty *boring* week.' I didn't want to bother Faith or Zoe with my problems.

Faith slugged me in the arm. 'I heard you busted Jesse for breaking the head off the statue!'

'Uhhhhhh, yeah, I sorta did. But he turned himself in.'

Zoe folded her arms and spoke like a concerned parent. 'That kid was really beating himself up over it,' she said. 'He was almost in tears when he told his side of the story to Principal Davis.'

'He seemed pretty upset yesterday too,' I said. 'I mean, I barely said a word to him, and he broke down like an old truck.'

'It doesn't make any sense,' Zoe said, frowning. 'So your project – it's finished and ready to be wheeled into the school, right?'

'Of course!' I said proudly. 'It's waiting for Principal Davis in the garage right now.'

'Cool,' Zoe said. 'I'll let him know.'

I smiled at Faith and Zoe, and then started walking towards the exit.

'Oh, and Chase?' Zoe called out.

I turned.

'Thanks,' she said, smiling.

Lifting my hand, I raised my thumb and jabbed it in the air towards her. I pushed open the door and stepped into the lobby.

 **Friday.
The lobby.**

School was starting in fifteen minutes, so students were beginning to swarm the halls.

The front office was just ahead of me. All I needed to do was catch a glimpse of the box Naomi mentioned to make sure that all three pieces of the statue were safely inside it. There were a few teachers inside the office, but not so many that I was worried about it. I just had to make it to the end of the hallway to where the principal's office was.

'Can I help you?' one of the office staff asked, leaning over the front counter.

I looked around, trying to figure out if the woman was talking to me.

'Yes, *you*,' she said, chewing gum with one side of her mouth. 'Is there something I can help you with?'

'Oh, um,' I said, stumbling. 'I'm just…uh…' and then I remembered that the nurse's office was right across the hall from the principal's. I held my stomach and made my voice sound sick. 'I'm not feeling too good…my tummy's, um…'

The woman pressed her lips to one side, nodding like she felt sorry for me. 'Someone's got soupy poopy?'

I had to bite the inside of my cheek to keep from laughing. I've never heard anyone say 'soupy poopy' before in my entire life, but I knew it was going to be my new favourite thing to say.

'Yup, soupy poopy,' I said with the best straight face I could muster. 'Soupy poopy…is what I have…'

The woman pouted. 'You poor thing,' she said, waving her hand down the hall. 'The nurse's station is there in the back. Have a seat on the bench outside her room. She'll be back in a few minutes.'

I nodded and hobbled down the hallway.

I passed some of the student counsellor rooms. The doors were shut so I figured I'd be safe if I put my ninja mask on. I always felt like I was better at stealth when I wore my ninja mask. Even if it was just in my head, that

was fine because it worked, and anything that helped me level up in stealth was okay by me.

At the end of the hall, I checked to see if there was anyone behind me. There wasn't.

The door to Principal Davis's office was wide open, but there wasn't anyone in it. His desk was in front of a giant bookshelf that had more plants on it than books. From where I was standing, I couldn't see the box.

I hated that I had to go *into* the room, but I had no other choice. And I had to act fast – Principal Davis could return at any second.

I stayed low to the ground as I worked my way across the carpet. The room had windows along the side that looked outside. One of the windows was wide open, so the room was freezing.

I left the door open in case someone might hear me shut it, but I wasn't too worried – there were no windows out to the hallway.

Sliding on my knee, I turned and stopped behind the principal's desk. His leather chair was pushed all the way in, tucked under the table.

Pushed into the small space where Principal Davis's legs would go was the cardboard box that Naomi had talked about.

I grabbed the box and dragged it closer. I pulled open the flaps and took a look inside.

Empty.

The box was *empty*.

'Looking for something?' came a voice from the hallway.

I freaked out and jumped up, which was a stupid mistake. Whoever was at the door was bound to see me wearing my ninja mask.

Luckily for me, it wasn't a teacher. Unluckily for me, it was a boy wearing a vulture masks. A Scavenger, and there was a whole bunch of his masked Scavenger friends behind him.

'Of course,' I sighed, feeling the air get sucked from my lungs. I'm not sure how the office staff missed a bunch of kids wearing creepy bird masks, but whatever.

A cold gust of wind slipped through the open window and washed over me.

'Where's the broken statue head?' I asked, my

voice shaking more than I thought it would.
After all this time, I was still freaked out by the
Scavengers.

'In a better place,' the boy in the mask said
with a muffled sound. 'Victor thinks keeping it
under the principal's desk is such a waste. It
should be out in front of the world for *everyone*
to see.'

'Out in front of the world?' I asked, stepping
around Principal Davis's desk, keeping it between

me and the Scavengers as they entered the room.

'Where it is doesn't matter,' another Scavenger said. 'All that matters now is that we're here with you, Chase.'

I didn't like how the Scavengers knew my name.

The girl reached for me. '*Join* us, Chase…' she hissed. '*Play* with us… forever…'

Uh, yeah, *super* creepy!

I backed up, until I hit the ledge of the open window. It was about waist height, and I gripped the ledge.

The Scavengers slowly moved forward, reaching out and wiggling their fingers slowly at me. The last time I had a run in with these kids, it wasn't nearly as creepy. Victor must've given the order to take their 'freak people out' game to the next level.

And I didn't even want to know what would happen if they actually got hold of me.

I raised my hand and pretended to tip a hat that wasn't there. 'G'day y'all!' I said, and then rolled out the window.

 **Friday.
Outside.**

As I landed behind the bushes outside Principal Davis's office, I could hear the Scavengers rush towards the open window, but they were too late. I was already crawling across the dirt along the side of the building.

Other students were just getting to school and walking towards the front doors of the building.

All I needed to do was take my mask off and wait for a break in the crowd so I could step out without being seen.

I watched, waiting for my moment, but it

didn't look like it was coming anytime soon.
The crowd of students grew thicker as the
seconds ticked by.

At that moment, someone clutched the
top of my mask. My hands flew up, grabbing
the bottom of the mask before it was pulled
off my face. I rolled onto my back so whoever
was holding onto me would let go.

I expected to see the Scavengers in the
bushes behind me, but instead it was a small
pack of red ninjas.

'You've gotta be kidding me,' I grunted,

shooting myself through the red ninjas, away from the front doors.

The red ninjas seemed to be everywhere all the time, but in the bushes outside the school? One of them *had* to have seen me fall out the window.

I figured I only had *minutes* to get into the school before they sent a mass text to the other red ninjas. I had to hurry if I didn't want an entire army chasing after me, trying to take my mask as some sort of prize.

I sprinted against the side of the building, not caring if anyone in the parking lot saw me that time. Getting spotted was better than getting caught by the ninjas who were hot on my tail.

'Just give us your mask!' one of the red ninjas ordered. 'That's all we want! Give it to us and we'll let you go!'

'Nope!' I hollered.

At the side of the school, I dug my foot into the dirt and dashed to my right, still running behind the bushes. The footsteps following me made me push even harder.

I wasn't sure where I was headed, but does anyone when they're getting chased by ninjas? Was that even a question that normal people asked themselves?

The side doors were coming up quick, but with my mask still on my face, I couldn't use them. My only shot was getting to the back of the school where nobody else was going to be, over to the dumpsters.

I slowed a little, but not so much that the ninjas behind me could catch up. They were still several metres away, and all I had to do was make sure I didn't trip over the spot where the footpath started.

At the doors, I leapt through the air, trying to clear the concrete walkway.

At the same time, someone forced open the doors, smashing them against me. My super heroic escape came to a stop in the blink of an eye, and I hit the ground.

I pushed myself up, staring at the dirty sneakers of the other kids standing nearby.

A few sneakers were caked in dirt – the

shoes of the red ninjas who had been following me.

But the sneakers from the other kids were clean – the ones who had opened the door.

I looked up and got an eyeful of something I'd never seen before.

Three kids hovered over me. All I could see were their eyes under their ninja masks – their *green* ninja masks.

The green ninjas' masks had two parts – a piece of cloth over the head, and a second piece of cloth tied around their eyes. They were wearing the kind of armour that motocross kids wear – the hard plastic shell that went over their chest and shoulders.

First red ninjas, and now green ninjas? Wyatt said I shouldn't be surprised if I saw a new ninja clan sprout up, but that was easier said than done. I *was* surprised.

And honestly, I held back a laugh. Red and green ninjas standing next to each other made it look like it was Christmas. I was being chased by Christmas ninjas!

GREEN NINJAS!
YOU'LL HAVE TO
TRUST ME AGAIN...
...THEY'RE
GREEN.

That only lasted about a second though because all six ninjas dove for my mask at the same time.

My mind went blank, and my muscles took over. I rolled away before any of the ninjas could touch me.

As they crashed into each other, I rolled to my feet, and started running across the grass.

A couple of adults stared from their cars as I dashed across the lawn. A few of them even raised their phones to take a pic. Being the ham that I am, I waved.

I cut around the last turn and saw the dumpsters in the distance. All I had to do was make it there so I could sneak in through the cafeteria doors. I just had to make it across the staff parking lot.

I ran hard, pumping my fists with each stride. The red and green ninjas were back in chase and they were gaining on me.

Slipping down the side of a bunch of SUVs, I thought that maybe I could lose them for a second. The dumpsters were too far away. I had to try something else.

Lowering myself onto the road, I scanned under all the cars. I saw twelve feet coming to a stop a few cars down.

'Where'd he go?'

'I don't know! He just disappeared!'

'He didn't just disappear, you dolt! He's here somewhere. He's just hiding.'

'What if he made it to the school already?'

'Good point. Let's split up. Red ninjas, search the parking lot. Green ninjas, check the dumpsters.'

'*Dangit*,' I said under my breath. 'Don't go to the dumpsters!'

I pushed myself off the road and bolted, trying to make sure all the ninjas saw me. I wanted them to chase after me. My only shot at the dumpsters was to get all the ninjas behind me.

'Hey, Christmas ninjas!' I bellowed, jumping up and down while I ran. 'Santa called! He's pretty unhappy that a bunch of his elves quit to become ninjas!'

Just as I'd hoped, all six ninjas started running after me again.

I was weaving through the cars and the ninjas split up behind me.

The ninjas were still on my tail, but my plan was working. The parked cars were perfect obstacles.

Suddenly, a group of Scavengers appeared from behind a dark green minivan.

I imagined what it would be like if my life were a video game. There'd probably be a banner saying, 'The Scavengers have joined your game!'

I skidded to a stop, looking back and forth between the ninjas behind me and the Scavengers in front of me.

Forcing myself to move, I ran and crouched between two parked cars, trying to get a grip on where I was in the parking lot. The dumpsters were much closer than I thought – only about twenty cars away.

And then I saw it – the cafeteria door, the one that led backstage.

Victor, all by himself, was wheeling my covered project through the door! He must have volunteered to take to the cafeteria for Principal Davis.

Victor caught me from the corner of his eye. When he turned to me, he laughed out loud.

I didn't waste another second. The ninjas and

the Scavengers were so close I could see their breath in the air behind the cars nearby. My sneakers hit the ground at a hundred kilometres an hour as I shot across the footpath.

The Scavengers were easy to lose first since their weirdo vulture masks messed up their vision. Most of them had to stop because they could barely see anything through the tiny eyeholes.

It was the ninjas I had to worry about.

There were only fifteen cars between me and the cafeteria doors. I ran fast, but the ninjas ran faster.

Ten cars to go.

They say you're never supposed to look behind you when you're racing because it'll slow you down. Whoever said that was right.

Glancing over my shoulder, I saw all six ninjas, like, right behind me.

That was it. I was toast.

It was impossible.

...

And then I realised the ninjas didn't want *me*. They wanted my *mask*.

I felt so stupid. I could just get another mask from my locker! I had tons of them!

Ripping my ninja mask off, I tossed it into the air like that lady at weddings who throws a bunch of flowers to her friends.

I slowed to a stop at the dumpsters since they were just outside the cafeteria. Catching my breath, I looked behind me.

There was nothing. The Christmas ninjas had disappeared, along with my ninja mask. The Scavengers were gone too, but I knew those guys wouldn't have gone far. If there was one thing I've learned since meeting the Scavengers, it was that they were never far away...

 **Friday.**
The cafeteria.

I waited until I wasn't breathing like a fat cat before entering the cafeteria. I didn't want to attract any attention, but after seeing the whirlwind of students in the room, I wasn't sure I could if I tried.

The cafeteria was so packed with kids that it was almost impossible to move around.

The stage curtain at the front of the cafeteria was shut. Zoe, Faith and Principal Davis were at the short staircase on the right side of the stage, nodding and talking. All three of them looked excited for the assembly to start.

The clock on the back wall said it was nine o'clock sharp, which meant that the curtains would open at any second.

Gidget, Slug and Brayden were standing against the wall right under the clock.

I jumped as high as I could a few times to see over the heads of the taller seventh and eighth graders. What was wrong with those kids? There were seats everywhere! Take a seat already!

Victor was nowhere in sight, but I didn't care. All I cared about was getting to my project. Victor wheeled it in, and I'm pretty sure it wasn't because he wanted to help out.

The three pieces of broken statue had been taken from Principal Davis's office, and after seeing Victor with my project, it didn't take too long for my brain to catch up. The broken head of James Buchanan was going to be somewhere on my project for the whole school to see when Principal Davis opened those curtains.

'Morning, Chase,' a voice said as I tried pushing my way through the crowd.

I turned around. It was Victor.

'You should find a seat,' Victor said. 'The show's about to begin.'

Victor held a bag of popcorn with one hand while stuffing his other hand inside it. I'm not sure if he was eating the snack or just running his fingers through it. Either way, it was weird.

'What did you do?' I said, pushing my way through the crowd towards him.

'You'll find out soon enough,' Victor said as he smiled. There were bits of half-chewed popcorn in his teeth.

'You said you weren't going to do anything like this!' I said. 'You told me your plan *wasn't* to make anyone hate me!'

The other kids around Victor and me started looking at us because of how loud I was.

Victor smiled while pressing his lips together. His eyes closed halfway as he raised his eyebrows. He sort of looked like a duck.

'I lied,' he said coldly.

Zoe's voice came through the speaker system.

'Alriiiiiiiiight, everybody!' she said into the microphone. 'It looks like it's about time for us to start, so if all of you could find a seat, we'll get things going!'

At once, everyone in the cafeteria started moving towards the chairs that were set up for the show.

I turned back to Victor so I could try and talk some sense into him, but he was gone.

Naomi was standing in the back of the room, filming the assembly on her new phone. When she saw me, she lowered her phone.

We stared at each other for what seemed like forever.

Finally, I mouthed the words, 'Help me!'

That's when Naomi looked away.

Most of the students in front of me, closer to the stage, had taken their seats. It was only me and a handful of other kids who were still standing.

Zoe was up the front with Faith by her side. I knew that Zoe didn't have a clue about what was going on, but I wasn't sure about Faith.

Was it possible that she was doing her own thing behind the scenes? Like, I had been working behind the scenes, but was Faith working *behind* behind the scenes? But the smile on Faith's face made me pretty sure she was clueless. She would have been too busy helping Zoe with the Bash.

Light peeked out from under the curtain, where the velvet fabric hung a couple of centimetres above the old wooden boards of the stage. The light stopped right at the centre, and then started a metre over again. That must have been my project.

I started pushing through the kids in their seats, trying my best to not look frantic. All I had to do was get to Zoe, explain the sitch, and then fix whatever Victor did to my project while the curtain was still closed. After that, everything could go on perfectly normally.

I was halfway across the room when Zoe spoke into the mic again. 'Students of Buchanan Schooooooool,' she sang. 'I'd like to welcome you to our assembly! As you know, our Bash is going to be held after school today, but we're here right now to get you *pumped*! We've got a little taste of what to expect tonight with some talent acts, games, and a couple of prizes, but first...'

Uh-oh.

Zoe grabbed at the thick, braided rope in front of the velvet curtain at the side of the stage, and starting pulling down on it.

I went into panic mode as I started racing through the crowd to get to Zoe before she opened the curtain.

Zoe laughed, huffing and puffing as she stopped pulling the rope. She pretended to wipe the sweat off her brow and the crowd laughed.

Faith grabbed the rope as well, and together they both pulled, putting all their weight into it.

The velvet curtain at the centre of the stage shook slightly, and then started parting slowly.

I turned towards the stage and started running faster. It was too late to stop Zoe and

Faith from pulling the rope, so the only other thing I could think of was to try and hold both sides of the curtain shut.

I flew to the front of the stage as the curtain split open a little more. My project was right behind the fabric and I could see what Victor had done.

The broken pieces of the statue were sitting on the sign at the very top of the entryway I had built.

I jumped onto the wooden stage, and grabbed both sides of the red velvet curtain, pulling them shut to keep my project hidden.

I used every ounce of muscle in my scrawny arms to get the curtain to shut again, but it was too late.

Zoe and Faith let go of the rope, gasping when they saw me. I probably looked like I was trying to be a class clown or something. I clenched my fists around the red velvet fabric, but the curtain was already opening on its own.

I refused to let go, but my arms opened so wide that it felt like my bones were about to break, and then I was thrown to the side of the wooden stage.

The crowd gasped when they saw the head of James Buchanan at the top of the entryway. I didn't move. I just let the sounds of all the angry voices fill my world as I stared at the project I had worked so hard on.

Victor had won. The Scavengers had won.

Through my blurry vision, I saw two kids climb on the stage towards me. When they were close enough, I saw that it was two hall monitors in suits.

Principal Davis took the broken pieces of statue off my project and cradled them in his hands. He looked at me, disappointed and shaking his head.

I slid off the stage onto the cafeteria floor. Everyone had been pretty upset about the broken statue all week, but I had no idea just how upset.

'How could you do something like that to our statue?'

'Don't you have any respect for President Buchanan's memory?'

'Take him away! Get him outta here!'

I started defending myself, but it was useless. The mob was so loud that nobody could even hear me.

Zoe and Faith stared, shocked, from the side of the stage.

I only hoped that Zoe would hear my side of the story before joining the club of kids who hated me, which at that point, was the entire

school. I'd kept everything about the Scavengers
a secret from Zoe, and I was beginning to think
that was a mistake.

How was it going to sound when I started
blaming a mysterious group of students that
almost nobody knew about? It would be like
blaming a bunch of ghosts!

I looked around at the faces of everyone
shouting at me. Gidget, Slug and Brayden were
still at the back. Naomi wasn't standing in the
spot where I had last seen her.

Victor was near the other end of the stage, shouting at me with the other kids around him.

He did it. He finished what the Scavengers started a few weeks back. I was defeated – *pwned.* If I was lucky, maybe I'd respawn at my old school... too bad that's not how real life worked.

I wasn't sure if there was any way I could come back from this total, utter humiliation. I'd have to switch schools, or grow a moustache...

... and then the microphone screeched with feedback as someone stomped across the stage.

The two hall monitors who were walking me out stopped in their tracks. Even Principal Davis spun around, covering his ears.

'*Chase didn't do this!*' someone yelled into the mic.

It was Naomi.

'Chase was set up by an eighth grader named Victor!' she continued quickly. 'Chase isn't the villain! He's not the bad guy that everyone thinks he is, and he doesn't deserve this hate!'

I stared at Naomi.

And then she dropped the bomb. 'Victor is the leader of the Scavengers!' The kids gasped. 'Yes, they're real, and they're a bunch of jerks!'

Victor dove towards the stage.

Naomi stepped backwards, but she was safe. The hall monitors who had been next to me grabbed Victor before he got too far.

Victor's earring dropped to the floor and bounced a couple of times. Some kids gagged when they saw it, but started laughing when they realised it was a clip-on earring.

Naomi held out her phone to Principal Davis. 'I've got all the proof on video. I filmed everything. Chase is innocent.'

The crowd of kids had quietened down. The only sound was Victor screaming about how Naomi was lying, but I'm pretty sure everyone could tell *he* was the one who was lying.

I was surprised that Victor wasn't trying to run away. I guess some kids just knew when they were beaten.

Principal Davis put his hand on my shoulder and asked me to wait in the lobby with Naomi so he could figure everything out with just the three of us. He set the pieces of broken statue on a bench right outside the cafeteria doors.

Victor finally calmed down as the hall monitors took him out of the cafeteria. He shot me a look of pure evil.

'This isn't over,' he said. 'This is just the beginning...'

'Nope,' Principal Davis said as Naomi stood by his side. 'It's over.'

Victor said nothing.

'Take him into the front office and have someone call his parents,' the principal said to the hall monitors. 'We're gonna get to the bottom of this if it takes all day.'

The two hall monitors nodded and took Victor away.

Principal Davis turned to Naomi and me. 'You two wait out here. I need to let Zoe know that she can continue with the assembly.'

A second later, the principal was gone, and it was just Naomi and me in the lobby.

There was a moment of silence before Naomi unzipped her book bag and took out the teacup that had been glued back together.

Handing me the teacup, she said, 'I want you to have this.'

'But—'

'No,' she said, interrupting me. 'I need you

to take it. I need for us to be friends again.
I need you to know how sorry I am ... for
everything.'

I stared at Naomi. She wore a smile, but also
looked like she was going to cry.

The teacup made a *CLINK* sound. Naomi
had put a stick of gold sparkly glue inside the
cup. She was giving me both.

'I needed to make things right,' Naomi said.
'A few weeks ago, during the election, I watched

you stand in front of the school, ready to sacrifice yourself to stop the Scavengers ... and when I saw you on that stage today, I knew it was my turn. It was the only way to make it up to you.'

I looked at the teacup in my hand. 'I'm not sure what to say...' I whispered honestly.

Naomi smiled. 'You don't need to say anything.'

Gidget, Slug and Brayden appeared in the doorway of the cafeteria. Zoe and Faith were on the stage, making jokes and performing skits for the rest of the students.

Gidget was texting, Slug looked half-asleep again, and Brayden ... was *smiling* at me.

'Why are you smiling like that?' I said to him. '*You're* the one behind all this! I saw those photos of you giving Naomi the statue!'

Brayden's smile disappeared. 'Oh, dude,' he said, shocked. 'I only did that because you said you wanted the Scavengers to make a move! Remember? You said it at the beginning of the week!'

'I ...' I said, and then stopped. '*What?*'

'He's right,' Gidget said, pointing at Brayden. 'I was there. You totes said that.'

'Oh, man,' I said, remembering. 'Dude, that was a *joke!*'

'Could've fooled us,' Gidget said. 'I thought you were serious too.'

I slapped my forehead as everyone laughed.

'So you guys are really done with the ninja clan?' I asked.

Slug stepped forward, wiping the sleep from his eyes. 'Are you kidding me?' he said. 'After that *insane* scene in the cafeteria? There's no way this thing is as boring as I thought! Forget the football team! I'm a ninja for life!'

'Good,' I said. 'Because I have a feeling things are going to get worse soon.'

They looked at me, puzzled.

'Let's just say,' I said, 'don't be surprised if you see another ninja clan pop up. I'm pretty sure we're about to have some big ninja problems.'

Gidget smiled. 'Nice.'

The principal stepped out of the cafeteria and let the doors shut behind him. He ordered Gidget, Slug and Brayden back into the assembly since there wasn't any reason for them to be in the lobby.

Principal Davis glanced at the door to the front office, and then said, 'Naomi, why don't you come in first, and explain exactly what in the world has been going on. I'll need to see the footage on your phone.'

Naomi smiled. 'Sure. I'll tell you everything, Principal Davis.'

'Chase, wait out here,' he said. 'I'll call you in after I speak with Naomi.'

I nodded and they both went into the front office.

Just like that, the lobby was empty. It was just the broken statue of President Buchanan and me.

I crashed on one of the benches out there, leaning against the wall, and let out a humongous sigh of relief. The weight of the Scavengers was off my shoulders, and I felt so light I thought I'd float away.

Brayden wasn't the bad guy I thought he was, and Naomi was back on my side.

I knew that I should've had hard feelings about Naomi, but I didn't. Those feelings were gone and I was happy to get rid of them.

Spinning the cup in my hand, I studied the spots where Naomi's dad had used gold-coloured glue to piece it back together. Naomi had called it *kintsugi*. The teacup was more beautiful because of its history – it was unique.

The friendship Naomi and I had was broken, cracked just like that cup, but Naomi was trying to glue it back together. I just needed to let her.

She used to be one of my best friends, but I suspected our friendship was going to be even stronger now because it had been glued back together.

That went for my ninja clan too. We'd been through a lot with a lot more to come, but it was stronger because of our struggle to survive as a team, and my own struggle to be a good leader. I might've lost my mask earlier that morning, but there was no way I was finished with being a ninja.

I felt unstoppable.

Whatever was going on with Wyatt and the red and green ninjas would show its ugly face soon enough. But I knew that with my best buds behind me, I could stand up to anything.

The glue stick inside Naomi's teacup clinked on the side. I took it out and opened it, studying the little sparkles.

The broken pieces of James Buchanan's head sat on the bench next to me, and I was struck with an idea...

Let's just say I fixed the statue.

Kintsugi!

Diary of a 6th Grade Ninja series

Collect the SET!

Marcus Emerson is the author of several highly imaginative children's books, including the 6th Grade Ninja series, the Secret Agent 6th Grader series, *Lunchroom Wars* and the Adventure Club series. His goal is to create children's books that are engaging, funny, and inspirational for kids of all ages – even the adults who secretly never grew up.

Marcus Emerson is currently having the time of his life with his beautiful wife and their amazing children. He still dreams of becoming an astronaut someday and walking on Mars.